FOREST MOUNTAIN

Arnie Buscomb is ambushed and shot by an outlaw trying to steal his horse. Wounded, he is befriended by a mysterious hermit lady, Caitlin Rourke. Marshal Lex Dexter is caught between a rock and a hard place when he encounters bounty hunters with wanted dodgers searching for Caitlin Rourke. Dexter must follow a dangerous trail which looks set to lead him straight to Boot Hill unless he can find some gunhands to get him out of trouble . . .

fry some of your trout. Mister, you got to eat.'

He started to shake his head, stopped abruptly and said, 'No thanks . . . I got to get back.'

'When you're ready, Mister Buscomb.'

He lay back looking up. 'Tomorrow.'

She didn't argue, she piled blankets atop him and would have given him the bottle but he held up a hand. 'No more, thanks all the same.'

She went outside to care for the horses, pitch feed and stand a while watching the tail-race of a shooting star. There were advantages to not having a man around and a disadvantage to having two of them at the same time, one who was hurt and another one who was a fugitive. One sure fact about fate, or destiny, was that when a person got out of bed in the morning, regardless of their plans, something totally unexpected would occur before darkness returned.

When she went back to the house, Luther was straining at his chains. He

23

stopped the moment she entered and pushed up a forced small smile. She said, 'You got all night, keep at it.'

Luther's reply was candid. 'I will. Them bastards from up north'll hang me if they can.'

From the bed, the storekeeper spoke. 'I'll help.'

Caitlin told Luther to lie on the bear rug near the fireplace and helped him hop that far, then she went to look at Arnie and he smiled at her. If he intended to speak she didn't give him the chance. She said, 'How did you know my name?'

'Saw it on an old dodger at the town marshal's office a year or so back. When you first come to the store I recognized you.' They exchanged a long look in silence before Arnie spoke again. 'Why'd you do it?'

Her reply was blunt. 'Go to sleep.'

She disappeared in a lean-to room. It was her bedroom. She locked herself in. The moment Luther heard the lock snap closed he reared up and addressed

24

the storekeeper in a loud whisper. 'You can get up. Get that army carbine over the mantle and . . . '

'Bullets?' Arnie asked cryptically. 'Horsethief, I owe her.'

'Nobody's goin' to hurt her. Keep the carbine handy while you're settin' me free.'

'And then what? You shoot us both?'

'No! I'll get on her horse an' you'll never see me again. I give you my word . . . Mister, if we go to that town tomorrow an' she tells the law down there what happened up here, sure as grass is green they'll lock me up an' contact folks up north.'

Arnie's reply was harsh. 'You tried to steal my horse. In this country that's a hangin' offence.' Luther was preparing to plead when the storekeeper added a little more. 'I told you, I owe her.'

'I'll be gone before she wakes up.'

Arnie eased up on to his side facing the log wall and that ended the conversation. Even if he'd wanted to free the fugitive in his present condition he wasn't able, and knew it.

Luther didn't give up. His loud whispering included begging, offers of money from a hidden cache, even an assurance he would leave the country and never return.

Eventually the storekeeper growled, 'Shut up, I'm tryin' to sleep.'

Luther worked until he was sweaty and could not get free of the chains. Eventually he fell asleep, was snoring in front of the cold fireplace when the tall woman returned to the parlour, ignored Luther and went to Arnie to ask if he was hungry.

He was. She built a fire in the cook stove with her back to both men when Luther awakened and said he had to go outside.

She ignored him until Arnie had been fed before removing the chains and taking him outside. When they returned, Luther was clearly upset.

'Posse riders,' he blurted out in Arnie's direction. 'A passel of 'em spread out near the foothills.'

Arnie looked at the tall woman, she inclined her head, rechained Luther and set about cleaning up after their meal, doing this in a unhurried, pensive way. The only time she spoke was when Arnie tried to sit up. She levelled a rigid finger and said, 'Lie down!'

Arnie continued to raise up. 'They'll most likely be lookin' for me.'

'*Lie down!*'

Arnie obeyed. He did it as awkwardly as he'd tried to sit up. He watched the tall woman's every move. She was methodical — and thoughtful. Both men kept their gaze fixed on her.

Eventually, she faced around and addressed the storekeeper. 'How long ago did you'n the town marshal see that dodger?'

'Well, a couple of years ago. It was you but now you got brown hair.'

'What did the marshal say?'

'He . . . I couldn't recollect where I'd seen you for several days. Not until you came for supplies. He didn't know you.'

'But you told him?'

'No. I didn't even tell my wife. I could've been wrong. I wasn't sure until you come back.'

She leaned on the table studying the storekeeper. 'Now then, when they get here it won't matter that I saved your bacon, will it?'

'I never saw you before except at the store. I owe you that an' more.'

Caitlin Rourke faced Luther, who had been listening with interest. She said, 'If they don't hang you, you'll send 'em back for me. Maybe you can make a trade with them.'

Predictably the fugitive swore he would never repeat what he'd heard as long as he lived.

Caitlin wagged her head. 'You'd lie if the truth'd fit better.'

'On my word, lady. On my mother's grave. Not a word to anyone. If there's a bounty on you, ma'am, your secret'll die with me. Take the chains off an' we'll never meet again. You got my word on it, ma'am.'

Caitlin considered Luther with a sardonic gaze until Arnie addressed the tall woman. 'If I don't tell 'em he was trying to steal my horse . . . '

'Maybe there's a dodger on him, Mister Buscomb.'

Arnie subsided. What she had suggested was indeed a possibility.

She continued to lean, arms folded. She was for a fact between the Devil and the deep blue sea. Arnie offered a suggestion.

'Tie his mouth closed, roll him into the other room. When they arrive . . . I fell down an' hit my head on a boulder, you came along and brought me here.'

Her reply to that was factual. 'There'll likely be someone among them, or down in Winchester, who's seen bullet creases.'

'Not bandaged like I am.'

She abruptly straightened off the table and turned in Luther's direction. Because she was a strong woman she hoisted Luther to his feet with little effort, herded him in the bedroom and poked him hard in the chest as she said, 'If you make a sound they'll find you. If they find you, no matter what you say, you're a horsethief and a wanted man up north for killin' a coach guard.'

Luther was sweating. 'Keep 'em out of the house.'

She latched the door from the outside as Arnie made a sound statement. 'He's got more to lose than you have. He'll be quiet.'

Caitlin made a pot of coffee, left the door partially open and sat at the table.

The storekeeper said, 'It'll be all right.'

She gazed at him. 'You can't ride back. It's too long a trip.'

Arnie disagreed. 'I can do it. I've *got* to do it. Not just for my wife but for the store. It's the only mercantile for miles. Folks depend on it.'

Caitlin made a slight smile. 'Next time go to one of the other lakes.'

He returned the smile without speaking.

They sipped coffee until one of the horses trumpeted then Caitlin went to stand in the doorway.

There were two of them. She thought she'd seen one of the men before down in Winchester. When they saw her they crossed straight to the cabin. She saved them from asking questions. 'Mister Buscomb is inside. He was over at Humbug Lake where he fell and hit his head.'

One of the men asked how badly the storekeeper was injured. She replied laconically. 'Lost some hair off the top of his head, bled some.'

'How did he get here, ma'am?'

'I found him over there and brought him here. Tie up, he'll be glad to see you.'

As the townsmen dismounted, one of them said, 'Not near as glad as his wife will be.'

Arnie was sitting up when the townsmen came inside. They greeted each other warmly before the storekeeper told them what the tall woman had done. 'I'd've likely died if she hadn't been over there and saw me fall in the rocks.'

The men eyed Buscomb. One said, 'Can you straddle a horse?'

Buscomb avoided Caitlin's gaze when he replied, 'Yes, I might need a little help up but I'm ready to go when you are.'

One of the townsmen faced the tall woman. 'We're real obliged an' his wife will sure be.'

Caitlin responded without any expression. 'I don't think he'd ought to make that ride. Not for another few days. He bled hard, he's weak . . . If you'd brought a wagon . . . '

One of the townsmen, a bull-necked individual with a neatly trimmed beard considered the storekeeper, then his companion. 'We could go back, tell his missus he's all right and come back with a rig.'

The second townsman was shorter and dark. 'How can a wagon make it up that goat trail?'

'He can ride down to level country,' his companion said, and faced the storekeeper. 'It's up to you, Arnie.'

Caitlin spoke before the storekeeper could. 'In a few days he'll be fit. For a fact he needs a doctor. If he tries to make that ride you'll bury him.'

The bull-necked man considered Caitlin in silence until he said, 'There's a doctor in Winchester. We could bring him up here.'

Caitlin slowly inclined her head. Her reason was personal reluctance about having visitors. But for a fact the storekeeper needed a doctor.

The bull-necked man interpreted her slight nod correctly and jerked his head for the dark man to follow as he went outside, reset his hat and considered the clearing, the corral where a mare got between her colt and the other horses and stayed there.

The dark man said, 'I've seen her in town with that bay mare.'

His companion was not interested in horses. He hoped the settlement doctor was down there; he was the only pill-pusher for miles and wasn't always where he should be when folks needed him. They rode out of the clearing side by side, disappeared where they entered the timber and kept on riding. Caitlin watched from the door. When they were out of sight she turned in the doorway looking at the store-keeper.

'I need those two days to think more'n you need them to get strong.'

'I told you, it's none of my business. I leave gossipin' to my wife. I got no idea about you at all.'

'Are you'n the town marshal friends?'

'We been friends for years. If you're thinkin' I'd pass the word about you, Caitlin, you're wrong.'

She left him to go out to the corral and lean to, to do some thinking. The storekeeper owed her, for a fact, but that wasn't something to rely on when there was a reward.

She pitched hay to the horses in separate places and went slowly back to the house.

Arnie was sitting at the table when she entered. He nodded without speaking as she went around opposite him and sat down. 'I've been three years building this house, clearing the land around it, ditching a spindly creek down here from higher up. This is where I belong, Mister Buscomb. This is where I've got everything I need. You maybe can't understand how much this place means to me.'

Arnie pushed the cup aside. 'I know, Caitlin. Believe me, I know. Life hasn't been a barrel of apples for you. You want some coffee?'

She arose. 'I'll get it.'

He waited until she returned with two full cups and sat down opposite him. He resumed where he left off. 'This is your special place. My special place is down yonder. I know about having a special place. As far as I know you're just a woman lives in the forest.'

'You know my name.'

'Well, I knew your name a long

time before you came to the store for supplies. I never used it, did I?' Arnie half drained his cup and grimaced, the coffee was strong enough to float horseshoes. He shoved the cup away.

'You got my word, Caitlin, what I stumbled across is your secret and my secret. You aren't likely to snitch and neither am I. Besides, I owe you. That weasel in the bedroom would have killed me. He thought he had . . . Caitlin? How did you knock him down?'

'With a slingshot I use for hunting small game.' She smiled. 'I have to take your word, Arnie, but I'll worry an' keep watch. If someone wearing a badge heads this way I'll saddle my mare and leave . . . it'll break my heart to leave this place.'

Arnie looked exasperated. 'Don't you believe me?'

'There's a reward, Arnie.'

'Is there? For a million in gold I might consider it. Not for anythin' less. *Caitlin, you have my word!*'

She arose. 'Take a little walk with me. You've got to do that every day until they come for you.'

He stood up: He'd had no trouble getting from the bed to the table. Nor did he have trouble reaching the door and going outside.

She watched him; when he faltered two-thirds of the way to the corral she pointed to a stump and he sat there looking around.

He had a question. 'Did you do all this by yourself?'

'Yes, and loved every minute of it.'

'Caitlin . . .'

'Let's walk.'

This time they reached the corral where the horses came over for nuzzling. The colt was wary. When Arnie held out a hand it ran to the far side of the corral. Its mother normally would have gone back there too. She didn't, she stood, eyes closed getting her neck scratched.

Arnie looked around. 'You cleared the land?' he asked.

'Yes. I'm going to clear more and make a split-log fence so the mare can run a little with her baby.'

Arnie studied the tall woman's profile and privately thought she should have been a man.

On the way back to the cabin he didn't have to rest. At sunset she made him walk again. He tired easily, otherwise he had no difficulty walking.

When they returned to the cabin she put a pot of water on the stove, got a fire lighted and said, 'Sit at the table. The bandage needs changing.'

Luther knocked on the locked door, he had heard what she said. When she unlocked the door he said, 'Take the chains off. I'm not goin' anywhere. an' I'll need that hot water and more clean rags, unless you want to do it?'

She didn't, so she hunted up clean cloth, took the hot water to the table and removed the chains.

3

Caitlin's Decision

Caitlin gave the outlaw her extra pair of boots and they fitted surprisingly well. Almost anyone else would have thanked her. Luther didn't.

The three of them went walking. Arnie in the middle and Luther making observations until Arnie told him he talked too much, then he was quiet.

The third day while Arnie was sleeping, Caitlin took Luther with her and went to a place she used often for gazing southward. There were huge old trees behind them, massive smooth boulders to sit on and while Caitlin sat with her knees drawn up with both arms around them, Luther fidgeted and talked. She was watching southward and only heard an occasional word. When they saw the light dray wagon with an outrider, Luther's fidgeting increased. He wanted to go back. She said they'd do that in good time; she wanted to see the two men on the wagon seat and the outrider. The little cavalcade was still a mile or better crossing in their direction over the nearly treeless expanse of grass country when Luther stood up. The tall woman told him to sit down. He made his second mistake with Caitlin Rourke, he swung a balled fist.

She came up to her feet in one lithe movement, dodged the fist and hit Luther twice, once in the midriff, the second time in the chest.

His eyes widened before he sank to his knees sucking breath. She waited but Luther was willing to believe he was no match for the tall woman.

He climbed back to his rock and did not move except to breathe shallowly.

The sun was climbing behind them where spiky treetops prevented sunshine from reaching down, except in a rare few places, and the light wagon got close enough to the abrupt rise of forested land to stop. The men palavered with the outrider. The driver talked up his hitch for the final drive, stopped when the only route upward was a trail wide enough for a horse but not if it was pulling a wagon.

This time the outrider dismounted and the three townsmen held another confab.

Caitlin stood up, dusted off and jerked her head. Luther followed her back in the direction of the clearing and the log house.

Caitlin kept Luther with her when she brought the storekeeper's big docile mare out to be cuffed first then rigged out. Daisy was left tied at the corral on the outside.

At the house, Arnie accepted the arrival of help almost stoically. His head hurt but the headache was gone. He went to the table, waited until the tall woman brought three cups of coffee, then said, 'Ma'am, anything I can do, let me know.'

She nodded and Luther said, 'He's comin'. You hear him?'

They did; a shod horse struck stones, a barefoot horse also stepped on stones but made no noise.

When the man appeared in the doorway, Luther gasped. He was wearing a lawman's badge on his vest. Arnie said, 'Come in Lex. This here is Luther. The lady is Mary Smith.'

The lawman nodded and asked the storekeeper if he could ride as far as flat land. Arnie nodded. 'I could ride the whole distance.' He suddenly remembered something. 'This is Town Marshal Lex Dexter, Winchester's lawman.'

The town marshal had even features, blue eyes and curly brown hair under his hat. He was powerfully built and about the same height as the tall woman. She offered coffee which he declined because, as he said, there were two men waiting down below with a wagon, and he'd like to get back to

Winchester before it got dark.

They went out where Daisy was waiting. Arnie toed into the left stirrup but faltered until the lawman gave him a boost.

Arnie looked down at Caitlin. 'I'd like to ride up someday,' he said, and she nodded about that. Luther fidgeted and kept the tall woman between himself and the lawman.

Marshal Dexter touched his hat-brim to Caitlin, kneed his horse and Daisy dutifully followed.

When they disappeared among the trees, Luther heaved a rattling sigh and Caitlin gave him a quizzical look. He was her remaining problem.

They returned to the house where Caitlin set about preparing a meal. Her silence troubled the outlaw. He tried making conversation but she remained silent.

She carried the plates to the table and sat down. As usual Luther ate like there was an impending famine. Caitlin picked at her food. Mid-way

through she looked steadily at Luther.
When he glanced up, saw her look he
swallowed hastily and said, 'I've got a
little money. I'd be glad to pay for a
bundle of food.'

She ignored the offer. 'Where would
you go?'

'Well, I got to have a horse. After
that in any direction but north. You
wouldn't sell the mare would you?'

'What would you do with a colt?'

'Leave it.'

'It's still sucking.'

'You could figure something.'

Caitlin shook her head, not at Luther's
ineptness but at his indifference. The
mare and colt were Caitlin's family.

Luther said, 'I got a hunnert dollars.'

'Keep walking until you find a ranch
that'll sell you a horse, Luther. When
you're astride don't come back. What
I should do is shoot you.'

Luther put down his eating utensils.
'You got my word. I'll never even
mention you.'

She arose to take the plates to the

cooking area. He twisted to watch and spoke again. 'I couldn't turn you in. You could say where I'm wanted. Besides, you been real decent to me.'

She didn't answer, but with the day ending she rechained him despite his loud, almost frantic promises and appeals. She chained him by one leg to the bed Arnie Buscomb had used and went outside where she didn't have to listen to him.

She fed the horses, sat on a stump listening to the mare eating and tried to think of what she should do. As she'd said, she could shoot Luther and if she didn't there was an excellent possibility that she would regret not doing it to her dying day. He was typical of his kind; he would lie and steal and because he knew there was a bounty for her, he would find an agreeable lawman and offer to split the reward, despite all his protestations to the contrary.

As long as he was alive she wouldn't be safe. She sat until moon-rise and every possibility she considered ended the same way.

She had shot a man once which was why there was head-money out for her dead or alive, but the circumstances had been totally different. This time it would be out-and-out murder. She had no stomach for that.

Luther was bawling like a bay steer so eventually she returned to the house. When she entered and saw him, had to listen to his repeated oaths and promises, his begging and whining she faced an obvious fact; since she dared not turn him loose she was going to have to spend her time listening to him as well as being watchful. Without a weapon he was harmless and after she'd hit him he knew she could fight like a man, but those things had little bearing on his presence.

Before she left him chained to the bed she told him that the following day they would go to the creek with a piece of lye soap and he would bathe.

That kept him briefly silent. The idea

of a woman standing by while he took an all-over bath kept him silent until she headed for her bedroom, then he swore with genuine indignation and threatened her.

She turned in the doorway, looked steadily at him until he was quiet, then passed through and barred the bedroom door from the inside.

Men like Luther Coyle who had lived by their wits had the instincts of coyotes, they did not yield with grace nor fail to scheme.

He spent hours working one of the legs off the bed. It was a wrist-sized scantling of dry fir. He put it back in place and tried to sleep. Eventually he did sleep.

He was still dead to the world when she emerged from the bedroom. He sat up eyeing her. He hadn't heard her lift the *tranca*, hadn't heard her at all until she was working at the stove. His plan to get her close enough to be hit over the head with the leg of the bed meant that he had spent half the night and a lot of exertion for nothing.

She put two plates on the table, knelt to free his leg chain and arose to jerk her head. So far she had not said a word and that bothered Luther.

As he ate, he complimented her on her cooking. In return he got a blinkless cold stare.

She removed the plates, brought back the coffee pot and refilled both their cups, still without a word.

Luther's apprehension increased by the moment. He made several attempts to get a conversation going and failed each time. Something was obviously holding her full attention. If he'd known it had to do with shooting him to ensure his silence he would have sweated bullets.

They were sipping coffee when the mare nickered. Both the people at the table sat up straight. The mare did not nicker again.

Caitlin arose to cross the room and open the door. A man she had met yesterday was standing there

48

with his fist raised to knock. They were both surprised. Behind Caitlin, Luther audibly gasped. The man in the doorway had a badge on his vest.

He smiled at the tall woman; they were nearly of an equal height, he may have been a couple of inches shorter. He fished a paper from a pocket and held it out. 'From Arnie Buscomb, ma'am.'

She accepted the paper and moved aside for him to enter. He seemed surprised to find a man at the table. He and Luther exchanged nods while Caitlin read the paper, lowered it and said, 'He don't have to do that, Marshal. He was hurt an' being the only person around I did what I could.'

The marshal softly smiled. 'Arnie's that kind of man, ma'am. He figured you saved his life so he sent that up here. A year's free of whatever you need. Mind if I sit down?'

He sat near Luther who was forcing a smile. Caitlin went after another cup and filled it. The marshal thanked her and raised the cup. As he put it down he said, 'I didn't know you was married.'

That stunned both Caitlin and Luther. After a moment she said, 'This here is . . . '

'Barney Noble,' Luther said quickly. 'A neighbour. Just come by to see if she needed anythin' from the settlement.'

The curly-headed lawman slowly nodded as he studied Luther. 'I didn't know there was anyone else livin' up in here, Mister Noble.'

Luther was glib. He had been all his mature life. 'My place is some distance north.'

'How long have you lived up here?' the lawman asked.

'Year, maybe a tad longer. Ain't that right, ma'am?'

Caitlin moved to refill the coffee cups and answered without looking at either man. 'Something like that . . . Marshal, I wouldn't feel right taking up the storekeeper's offer. Free supplies for a year, that's likely to be an awful lot.'

Luther's eyes jumped to Caitlin. Before he could speak, if that had been his intention, the marshal arose. 'It's a long ride, ma'am.'

'All the way up here to give me the letter?'

The lawman went to the door before replying. 'We're friends, ma'am.' As though that was an adequate explanation, the lawman went over to his horse with Caitlin following. As he was tightening the latigo she said, 'Did Arnie tell you about Barney Noble?'

The marshal faced her and nodded without speaking. He then mounted and touched his hat-brim as he rode southward in the direction of thick stands of timber.

Luther bellowed. Caitlin headed for the cabin but not immediately.

Luther was understandably upset. He abruptly said, 'I got to get away from here. That lawman looked at me funny. That damned storekeeper told him about me as sure as I'm settin' here.'

Caitlin sat at the table. The storekeeper had given his word he would tell no one about her, but he hadn't done that with Luther.

For a number of reasons she could agree that getting rid of Luther Coyle would be beneficial. The man was raffish, conniving, a willing and capable liar — and he knew her secret.

She made a bitter choice; she had worked like a slave creating her peaceful and private bit of the world but with Luther gone she would have to abandon her special place. He knew there was a reward for her apprehension and she had not a shred of doubt that as soon as he could and if he could locate either a lawman or a bounty hunter and lead the way back to her cabin and clearing, he would do it.

She made the decision, what it would cost her was in her face when she said, 'I'll make you a bundle,' and went to the cooking and storage area.

He watched her with bright eyes. 'I'm beholden to you,' he exclaimed. 'You can shuck the loads out of my gun when you give it back to me.'

She said nothing for as long as was required to make the bundle of food which she wrapped in a faded small towel and walked over to hand it to him as she said, 'You'll steal a horse somewhere, an' you can get another gun the same way.'

She removed his leg-chain and went to the door with him. Her last words were, 'There's a scrap of soap. Take a bath, Luther.'

She did not say she wished him well.

He stood a moment looking in the direction of the corral. She shook her head. 'Walk, Luther. Don't come back. *Go!*'

He went around the side of the house and across the clearing. When he had disappeared in the timber she went to the corral to talk to her mare. Later, she went into the clearing and sat in the grass looking back toward the log house it had taken her more than a year to build.

There were bees in the grass and beyond among the forest's fringe a pair of quail called.

She did not return to the house until evening chill arrived. She built a fire and sat at the table until full dark was down. There were places she could go but not deeper into the mountains; it had to be some distant country and start over.

She was sick at heart but felt no pity for herself.

She had hunted and explored the mountains in three directions. She was familiar with all the lakes, had fished them all.

She knew the glades, the natural secret places, even the streams where she'd panned gold.

Possibly no one knew Forest Mountain as well, certainly not Luther who walked until he was tired and found a small clearing with an ancient deadfall fir on the far side where he gathered dead limbs for a fire. He expected to stay warm until daylight. When his horse had gotten away it had taken not only his saddle but his bedroll.

The sun was still casting light when he made his fire, opened the food bundle and ate. He hadn't crossed a creek since leaving the tall woman's place but he would find water.

He would also find a horse. In this kind of country there were homesteaders who built close to woodlands from which they got the logs for their shacks, barns and corrals. He would angle southerly, downhill but remain high enough to see where there was a house, or a ranch yard.

He had money which the tall woman had not asked about. His clothing was faded and soiled. He would appear to be a down-at-the-heel rangeman, moneyless and hungry, unshaven and unshorn.

He smiled into the little smokeless

fire. He had more money than most folks made in a year.

He heard what sounded like a foraging bear. He scarcely breathed. Without a weapon, if it was a boar bear or a sow bear with a cub . . . He stood up and did not move. The sound came from the north-east. It sounded like a large animal ploughing through underbrush and fir saplings, and it was coming in the direction of his small clearing.

There were big old shaggy fir trees he could climb. He cursed the tall woman for keeping his gun.

It was a bear! He heard it rear up and make a bellowing growl. There was a single gunshot and afterwards the sound of a large animal crashing its way through whatever was in the path of its retreat.

Luther seemed fixed to the ground even when a horseman worked his way among the forest giants toward the clearing.

Luther thought of running, of hiding.

56

When the horseman saw his fire he would know someone had been there. On horseback he could sashay until he found Luther.

The rider passed between two immense trees and Luther recognized the Winchester lawman and didn't know whether to feel relief or fear.

The marshal nodded, stopped with both hands on the saddlehorn and said, 'I followed you from the cabin. Do you have a gun?'

'No.'

The marshal dismounted as he said, 'Good,' and stood trailing his reins gazing at Luther. 'Mister, I hunt these uplands every buck season. I knew where the woman's place was an' I knew she didn't have any neighbours. Somethin' else, Mister Barney Noble: Arnie said your name was Luther the first time I came to the cabin. Mister, you're wanted somewhere.'

Luther snarled, 'That damned storekeeper!'

The lawman ignored the anger,

swung back astride and said, 'Walk. Due southward.'

'To where?'

'To Winchester, the place you can see from the tall lady's place. Walk, Mister Noble!'

Before Luther moved, he spitefully said, 'That tall woman back yonder is wanted. There's a bounty on her.'

'Walk! I'm not goin' to tell you again, I'll ride right over the top of you.'

Luther started walking but glancing back as he told all he knew about the tall woman.

The lawman waited until Luther was talked out then he said, 'If you were tellin' the truth I wouldn't be interested in splittin' the reward.'

Luther was occupied picking his way through the forest where there was no sunlight, never was. Only when they halted on the downslope course and could see open grassland did he speak again.

'There's likely a big bounty on her,

Marshal. I can tell you for a fact she can use her fists like a man an' she's mean. Real mean.'

The lawman's response was, 'Let's go, Mister Noble. It'll be past suppertime if we don't hurry.'

4

How Things Were

It was a long walk and Luther alternately whined and complained. He also repeated what he knew about the tall woman and sneered when he said, 'Your storekeepin' friend lied when he said her name was Mary Smith. It's Caitlin Rourke, an' he knew it.'

By the time they saw a sprinkling of lights, the moon was climbing, and until he was herded to the coach road Luther complained about encountering rocks he could not see.

On the outskirts of Winchester, he halted and faced around.

'This is your last chance to get rich, Marshal. She's got a big bounty on her and she's got a cache hid in the cabin.'

The marshal swung his romal lightly

and urged his horse forward. Luther's shoulders stung from the swung romal and as he entered the town from the north he was killing angry.

Winchester's jailhouse was old but well maintained. It had one large cell and two smaller ones. Marshal Dexter went over Luther for hide-out weapons, found none and herded him to one of the small cells.

As he was locking the door he said, 'You're wanted in a border town between Montana and Canada. Which is it?'

'Go to hell. Here, I offered you a chance to retire an' you . . . '

'Sleep well. I got a bad memory, sometimes I forget to feed prisoners for several days. Good night, Barney Noble.'

Winchester was one of those grass country settlements that grew from a buffalo hunter's camp to a town with business establishments on both sides of a wide roadway. Along with having a church, it also had an apothecary shop owned by an elderly gnome addicted to celluloid collars, a physician's place complete with an immaculate examination room which was also where emergency surgeries were performed by a medical doctor whose specialty was internal medicine not surgery. There was no other medicine man for over a hundred miles.

The largest and clearly the most thriving business in Winchester was the emporium. As with the physician, there was no other general store for a hundred miles. Rebecca Buscomb had managed the store during her husband's absence and even after he was brought back to town and the doctor sewed his scalp and loaded him with laudanum she continued to run the store for a week.

How he had been injured was a topic of local interest. Rebecca stated emphatically that she would not allow him to go up yonder fishing alone ever again. Winchester, with no reason to do otherwise, accepted the story of Arnie's injury being the result of slipping on the soggy bank of Humbug Lake and striking his head on rocks.

All but Nathan Bedford, the physician, who shaved only when his face itched, who played poker at the saloon and drank, and who was a shrewd individual, which he proved the day after the marshal returned with a prisoner.

Nat Bedford arrived at the jailhouse smoking a fragrant cigar and put a steady gaze on the marshal at his desk when he said, 'Lex, the only way Arnie could've got that crease on his head would be if he stood on his head over a very pointed, sharp rock, an' even then I'd have found bits of stone flakes and dirt in the wound.'

Doctor Bedford removed the cigar and studied it. 'That wound came from a bullet crease or I'm the Angel Gabriel.'

Lex Dexter accepted this without commenting, except to say, 'The hermit lady would know. She's the one who found him and brought him to her cabin to care for.'

The doctor flicked ash before speaking again. 'Would she shoot Arnie?'

The marshal doubted it but said he would ride up yonder and talk to her. Doctor Bedford arose, plugged the cigar back into his face and said, 'Two inches lower an' Rebecca would have been a widow.' As an afterthought, while standing in the doorway, the physician also said, 'Be right careful, Lex. From what I've heard . . . Be right careful.'

The marshal and Arnie shared a conviction; for that long a ride a person had to be in the saddle while it was still dark.

He made arrangement for the caféman to feed his prisoner until he returned, something the caféman did willingly because he could bill the town council for payment.

It was cold as well as dark when he left Winchester. The caféman hadn't been pleased at having to serve a breakfast only minutes after he'd fired up his stove. The marshal smiled to himself. The caféman was naturally grumpy, but he was a good cook. In fact he was the only professional cook in Winchester.

The marshal mulled over what Doc Bedford had told him and before dawn light, with Forest Mountain a massive etching of darkness that obliterated stars, he left town. For several hours it was too dark to see much, nor was there much he hadn't seen often before until he could make out the dark and formidable massif of Forest Mountain.

As he was working his way up the dog-leg of a trail he heard a horse whinny. The sun was rising which for most folks meant it was chore time. When he was passing among among huge old trees and could see the cabin in its clearing, he also saw the tall woman in her pole corral scratching the colt while the mare ignored them both to scarf up breakfast hay. He whistled and the woman whirled. As he left the timber behind he raised his right hand in a friendly gesture and she climbed out of the corral, stood outside it and waited. In new-day light she looked impassive and did not return his salute.

He rode directly to the corral and swung down to loop his reins, turned and said, 'Good mornin'.'

The woman returned the greeting, studied the lawman briefly before saying he must have left Winchester in the dark, which he admitted was true. Then she said, 'I've got the coffee pot on the stove. Have you eaten?'

He had, but knowing what she was going to say next he told her he could eat any time, and she led the way to the house.

There was a corresponding warmth inside in contrast to the morning chill outside. She went to her cooking area to rassle a meal. Lex Dexter draped his hat from a set of antlers, sat at the table and watched her. Clearly she was not comfortable in his presence, and just as clearly she was not given to unnecessary talking, so he offered openers when he said, 'Do you know Doctor Bedford in town?'

She was sliding eggs and fried meat on to a pair of plates when she replied, 'I don't know him but I've seen his shingle out front.'

She did not look at the marshal as she placed the plates opposite each other and put eating utensils close by.

When she had filled their coffee cups he said, 'Someday I'd like to live as you do, private an' in a settin' like this. Warmth in the winter, shade in the summer.'

She looked straight at him. 'Town folks wouldn't like what has to be done, clearing land, building, storing up for winter.'

'Some,' he admitted, 'wouldn't.'

The eggs were golden brown, wild honey made them delicious. Between mouthfuls he said, 'I'd like to ask you a personal question. Why did you go

67

to all the work to make this little scrap of paradise? In town . . . '

'In town, Marshal, a person can feel cramped.'

He said no more until he had finished his second, and best breakfast, then as she was clearing the table he asked another question. 'Doc Bedford said the storekeeper didn't get hurt by fallin': he said that slit in his scalp came from a bullet.'

She returned with the pot to refill their cups and again sat opposite him. 'Luther, or Barney Noble, shot at him when he was fixing to steal Mister Buscomb's horse.'

'An' you . . . ?'

'I was out rabbit hunting with my slingshot; cheaper than bullets. I saw what was happening. After Luther fired I hit him in the back of the head with a rock from my slingshot.'

The marshal sipped coffee gazing at the tall woman. When he'd emptied the cup and put it down he said, 'When I was a kid I went huntin' with a slingshot. After a lot of practice I got pretty good.'

The tall woman put her coffee cup aside looking steadily at the man across the table. 'Is that why you made the ride up here, Marshal, to find out how Mister Buscomb got hurt?'

Dexter's gaze swept past her to the door and back before he answered. 'Not altogether, ma'am.'

'I didn't think so. Why else did you come?'

'Well, that weasel calling himself Barney Noble told me an interestin' story.'

'About me?'

'Yes'm.'

'So he came into town?'

'No, I took him prisoner after he left here.'

Her eyes narrowed slightly and her nostrils flared. 'Marshal, I had a choice: shoot him, bury him where he'd never be found or let him go. He swore up an' down he'd never utter a word.'

'And you believed him?'

'No, but, shootin' someone in cold blood . . . you understand?'

The marshal nodded. Before he could speak she also said, 'What he told you is true, there's five hundred dollars on me in Montana for killing a man.'

Marshal Dexter leaned back in his chair considering the tall woman. Again, she spoke before he could. 'You came up here to find out if that weasel's story was true and if it was to take me back, five hundred dollars' worth.'

Lex Dexter was learning something about the tall woman, she was blunt. He asked another question, 'Where in Montana, ma'am?'

'About five miles north of Button-willow.'

'Go on,' he said quietly, and she made a little fluttery gesture of futility with her hands before continuing.

'His name was Jess Ames. His father owned half the town as well as the bank — and the law.'

'You didn't shoot his father.'

'His son, Jess Ames. The Ames got lots of money and own a big cow outfit, hire four year-round riders. The old man's wife died three years ago.'

'Old, was she?'

Caitlin Rourke gave her head a vigorous negative head shake. 'She fell from a horse and broke her neck.' The steady gaze narrowed again slightly. 'Marshal, she drove horses but seldom rode them. I know because we were close. She was scairt of horses.'

'What did the doctor say, ma'am?'

'There was no doctor. She died on a Tuesday an' they buried her on a Thursday.'

'What did folks say?'

'I told you, the Ames owned most of the town. A neighbour told me she was dead, and the dead are best left buried. He was right about that; maybe there was wonder but it never was mentioned. But I do know they loved each other.

'Jess was like his pa, overbearing, born with a mean streak, but when he was of a mind he could charm a bird down out of a tree . . . He cracked my jaw. A year later when he was mean drunk he kicked me on the floor so's I couldn't stand straight for a week. The last time he hit me in the side and broke three ribs.' The tall woman exhaled and inhaled deeply. 'The next time when he was mean drunk and came after me with a scantling from the wood box . . . I shot him.'

'Why didn't you tell the law?'

'I told you, the Ames owned the law.'

'Couldn't you have run for it?'

'Where? I was his wife. Any place I ran to would side with a man against the word of a woman. So, I bought my mare and left in the night riding south. Marshal, this is where I ended up, on Forest Mountain, built my house and kept to myself. I hoped I'd be given time to rebuild my life . . . Care for more coffee, Marshal?'

He ignored the question, went out front, built a smoke and was sitting on a stump near the corral when she came out carrying a bundle wrapped in a blanket. She said, 'I'll turn the mare out an' hope wolves don't find her baby. Marshal . . . ?'

He tipped down his hat to avoid direct sunlight. 'Does anyone besides my prisoner know your story?'

She put the bundle down before saying, 'By now he'll have told half the territory.'

'No, ma'am. He's locked up.'

'The storekeeper knows.'

'Arnie? You kept him alive. I've known Arnie Buscomb a lot of years. He'd never mention what he knows even to his wife, maybe especially to his wife.'

She stood hip-shot regarding him. He met her gaze with no effort as he said, 'I had a sister named Edna. We grew up close as peas in a pod. She married a Texan named Hardesty. Travis Hardesty . . . He killed her.'

The tall woman shifted stance. Marshal Dexter told her the rest of it. 'I hunted him down and shot him three times, twice through the soft parts an' some later through the head.'

She eased down on her bundle. She was wise enough to know this was a time to be quiet. When he eventually stood up her mare and his gelding were snapping at each other over the top corral stringer.

Caitlin Rourke said, 'He's thirsty. I'll take him to the creek.'

He remained on the stump watching his horse being led to water. He had just told another living soul something he hadn't told anyone in over fifteen years.

When she returned, she avoided his gaze as she handed him the reins and leaned to hoist her bundle. He said, 'No, stay here,' and without another word he swung astride and rode across the clearing, riding on a loose rein.

She went back inside with her bundle, left it on the parlour bed the storekeeper had used and went back over to the corral to talk to 'her family', the only family she had.

Dusk was fading into night by the time Marshal Dexter reached Winchester. He left his horse to be cared for with the liveryman, went over to the café hungry as a bitch wolf and the caféman said, 'That prisoner of yourn is crazy as a pet 'coon. I never heard so much bull in my life.'

The marshal made a wry smile. 'Some folks will lie an' make up stories when the truth would fit better.'

'What'll you have?'

'Anythin' you got that'll go down an' stay down.'

It was late for the supper trade, the café was empty except for the town marshal. The caféman called from his kitchen, 'You know that tall woman who lives on the mountain?'

'What about her?'

'That shifty-eyed, unwashed, son of a bitch told me the wildest tale about her . . . You can fill your own cup, Marshal. Go behind the counter and he'p yourself. He said he'd give me three hunnert dollars to set him free. He also said you trumped up a charge, that he's never broke no laws.'

When the meal came, the caféman placed it in front of the lawman and snorted. 'I've run across some first-class ringers in my time but that scrawny son of a bitch . . . What's his name, Marshal?'

'Calls himself Barney Noble.'

'That ain't his name?'

'No. It's Luther Coyle.' As the marshal spoke he raised an amused glance and said, 'Three hundred? That's more'n I've been offered.'

The caféman stood, arms crossed, leaning on the pie table opposite the marshal. 'Fellers like him, his folks'd've done better to pinch his head off an' raise calves on the milk.'

The marshal felt better with the pleats worked out of his stomach. His parting comment to the caféman was: 'Alec, you got to learn to trust.'

As the door closed, the caféman loudly snorted.

The marshal lighted the hanging lamp in the office then went down to look in on his prisoner. The unwashed prisoner's appearance hadn't improved as he gripped the straps of his cell and said, 'There's a big reward for that woman, did you know that?'

Lex Dexter ignored that to ask a question. 'How'd you get this far south, by stealin' horses as you went?'

'Me, steal horses? I never stole no horse in my . . . '

'What were you goin' to do with the storekeeper's mare?'

'That's different, I'd been afoot a long time goin' through some pretty rugged country.'

'An' they were behind you?'

'Somewhere behind me. Only I'd covered a lot of territory. It's a good chance they turned back long ago.'

'Not,' the marshal said, 'if they're any good at trackin' and reading sign.'

He returned to the office when he heard someone open and close the roadway door. After closing and barring the cell-room door, he nodded to his visitor and went to sit behind his desk. He was tired; a full stomach hadn't noticeably re-energized him.

Arnie Buscomb sprawled in a chair. He too was tired. He was still recuperating and this day his wife hadn't stepped foot inside the store. He showed a weary smile as he said, 'Did you go up yonder today?'

Lex Dexter nodded. 'She was right grateful for your offer of whatever she'd need at the store.'

That wasn't why the storekeeper had come over to the lighted jailhouse. He said, 'I had a couple of strangers at the store this afternoon. Didn't talk much but asked questions about the local law and if maybe I'd seen the person they showed me a picture of.'

The storekeeper unfolded a worn dodger and arose to spread it flat on the marshal's desk. They both gazed at the picture and Arnie read the printing below and said, 'Her hair was lighter, otherwise . . . '

Marshal Dexter gazed at the face on the wanted dodger and speculated how badly a wealthy man named Ames wanted the killer of his son.

He reared back from the desk looking at the storekeeper and asked a question. 'How's your head?'

'About healed. I don't expect the hair'll grow back but I can comb over it. Marshal . . . ?'

'If the strangers are still around I'll look them up in the morning.'

Buscomb carefully folded the dodger. 'They wanted to post it in the window.' He sighed. 'I don't think I can make that long a ride yet, but she'd ought to be warned.'

Marshal Dexter didn't want to make that long ride either, but that wasn't how he was thinking. 'If they come to the store let me know, Arnie.'

'I will. You got anything particular in mind?'

'Keep between them and the tall woman.'

'Marshal, they'll likely go to the

eatery before visiting the store.'

Dexter nodded. He had already considered that possibility, and after the storekeeper left, he blew out a long breath, shook his head and locked up from out front for the night.

5

How Not to Make Friends

In the morning he missed them. The caféman said two strangers had eaten earlier. He had no idea where they might be but the liveryman told the marshal the pair of strangers had ridden out before sunrise. He didn't know which direction they had taken.

There was the possibility that they might have heard about the tall woman; it was common knowledge where she lived although little else was known about her.

He got his horse and went tracking. The initial problem was that the manhunters' tracks, if they had gone north, were intermingled with dozens of other shod-horse tracks in the roadway.

He rode several miles in the direction

81

of Forest Mountain looking ahead in the open country for movement, and saw none. He was tempted to go up yonder, but with no valid reason to believe the strangers had gone in that direction, he rode westerly for no reason except that if the manhunters were cruising the countryside they might have gone that way.

He had to sashay back and forth a mile or so north and south to cut sign if there was any, and there wasn't.

He headed back for town, did not meet a soul on the way until, a half-mile or so from the roadway, he watched a northbound stage raising dust.

Back in Winchester he went among the business establishments. No one, even at the saloon, had seen a pair of strangers, but his enquiries roused interest and inevitably the small town moccasin telegraph functioned; Marshal Dexter was seeking two strangers.

One of the last places he visited was Buscomb's store and both Arnie and his domineering wife shook their heads. There had been no sign of the strangers.

Rebecca said, 'They wanted Arnie to post a Wanted poster in the window and since he didn't do it I expect they'll be back to ask why.'

At the jailhouse, Dexter went into the cell room. His prisoner was lying full length on his cot and reared up to complain about not having been fed.

The marshal ignored that. 'There's a pair of bounty hunters in town, rode in yesterday.'

The man calling himself Barney Noble reacted. 'They got to have extradition papers, Marshal.'

Lex Dexter's reply was curt. 'Maybe they have. I haven't seen them yet.'

'Marshal, you got first rights.'

'Have I?'

'Sure, I was fixin' to steal the storeman's horse, wasn't I?'

The marshal returned to his office briefly before going to the eatery for two pails of food for his prisoner. When he got back and was unlocking

83

the door after telling his prisoner to go stand by the back wall, the weasel-eyed man said, 'Whatever bounty they got on me, I'll double it if you don't let 'em take me.'

Dexter put the pails on the cot and locked the door after himself without saying a word. The prisoner called after him. He only had to listen until he closed and barred the cell-room door, then the prisoner's noise was shut out.

He was worried and restless. If those manhunters were as seasoned at their trade as he thought they had to be if, after all this time, their search had led them to Winchester, possibly they were simply visiting towns to leave dodgers, but Dexter didn't believe that.

He had believed they either had reason to be in the Winchester country or had followed sign and either knew or suspected Caitlin Rourke was in the area.

He had doubts about that possibility because he had seen no sign of horsemen heading toward Forest Mountain.

It was a long, anxious day and he wandered the town for some indication of the whereabouts of the strangers. When he visited the bear-built blacksmith, the bald proprietor told him two strangers had come by yesterday to have their animals reshod. He was so far behind in other work he'd told them to return in a day or two. His last remark was consistent with a blacksmith's work. He told the marshal the animals of both strangers needed hoof trimming as much as they needed reshoeing.

The only description he had of the strangers came from Arnie Buscomb. 'About your height, don't say a word they don't have to say. Looked to me like rangemen. They was both of a size without no expression and eyes that never left a person they was facing.'

It was a good description. The marshal was at the eatery having an early supper when the caféman leaned across the counter, poked Dexter and jutted his jaw.

A pair of riders were passing the caféman's roadway window riding on a loose rein in the direction of the livery barn. Their animals were leaned-down to bone and muscle, their saddles showed signs of long use except for the saddle-bags, they were newer, army issue, larger than built-in saddle-bags usually were.

The men were different yet alike. They rode against the cantle the way professional horsemen rode, their clothing was faded, the hats had sweat stain and both men needed shearing and a shave.

Dexter left his meal to stand by the window and watch them turn in and dismount at the livery barn. As he watched the hostler lead their animals away, one of them jerked his head and said something which was indistinguishable to Dexter, but when they angled across the roadway in the direction of the eatery, Marshal Dexter returned to the counter and resumed eating.

The strangers beat off dust before entering the eatery. When Dexter looked up they nodded and went further along the counter. He nodded back and ate more slowly.

It was in the caféman's favour that when he came out of his cooking area and saw the strangers, he showed no expression as he walked past the marshal to take their orders.

One of them had the accent of Texas. His companion not only lacked an accent, when he spoke it was curt and incisive.

As the caféman was heading back for his cooking area he lowered and raised one eyelid as he passed the lawman.

Marshal Dexter, professional lawman or not, had an easy and amiable disposition. As he was raising his coffee cup he spoke to the only other patrons of the eatery.

'You boys new to the country?'

The curt man turned a testy glance.

'We might be. Who are you?'

'Town Marshal. Name's Lex Dexter.'

The testy-tempered man's voice softened a little as he said, 'We was goin' to look you up. My name's Art Waters. This here is Will Roberts.'

Dexter nodded, the strangers nodded back and the testy man spoke again. 'We're lookin' for a tall woman who murdered a man up north. I got some dodgers in my saddle-bags; we'll bring you one directly. Meanwhile, if you know the country you can likely help us.'

The Texan grinned. 'An' we need he'p. We been ridin' for a month. I'm gettin' calluses.'

Dexter went back to his meal. 'Help you any way I can. Tell me about this woman you're lookin' for.'

'Her name's somethin' like Catbird. Her last name's Ames. She shot her husband in cold blood. There's bounty on her.'

'What does she look like?'

'Tall for a woman, blonde hair.

Tougher'n a boiled owl. We never met her but the feller we hired out to, Carl Ames, was father to the feller she murdered. He hired us to find her'n fetch her back.'

Dexter pushed his empty platter aside. 'If you find her down here . . . '

'We'll take her back to Mister Ames.'

Dexter considered his coffee cup. 'You'll need an extradition order.'

The testy man named Waters looked stonily at the marshal for a moment before replying. 'We wouldn't think of doin' it any other way.'

Dexter dropped coins, stood up, nodded and left the café. When he got back to his jailhouse office, Arnie Buscomb was waiting. He was wearing his store apron rolled up and tucked under his belt. He was sweating. When the marshal walked in, the storekeeper seemed startled. Obviously his mind had been elsewhere.

Dexter went to a wall bench, sat down and thumbed back his hat. 'Are you all right?' he asked.

Buscomb arose, went to the desk and placed some rolled-up papers on the desk. Dexter crossed over and unrolled the papers. There were four of them and they were all the same as the one Arnie had showed Dexter a day or so earlier: Wanted posters with an excellent likeness of Caitlin Rourke broadly displayed with the amount of bounty money below.

As the marshal turned, the storekeeper reddened. 'In the saddle-bags of one of 'em.'

Dexter returned to the bench eyeing Buscomb and gently wagged his head. The storekeeper's response to this was defensive. 'She saved my life.'

'How'd you happen to go search their saddle-bags?' the marshal asked.

'They come here to get her. They gave me one of the dodgers to put in the roadway window. Well, a man wouldn't have to be real *coyote* to figure they'd do what they could to find her, an' like I said, I owed her, so . . .'

'So you went to the barn, took those dodgers, Arnie, that's about the same as tellin' them she's hereabouts an' someone's set against them findin' her.'

The storekeeper wiped his face with a large handkerchief before speaking again. 'If I'd left them dodgers where they were an' they showed 'em around the territory, specially here in Winchester . . . I'll tell you again; I owe her. If I can throw a little dust in their eyes I'll do it.'

Thin-lipped, ramrod-straight Rebecca Buscomb appeared in the doorway, ignored the lawman and said, 'Arnie, we got customers!'

Buscomb threw a final look in the marshal's direction and followed his wife across the road.

Marshal Dexter didn't have as much time to think as he expected to have. The pair of manhunters appeared in his doorway and this time the amiable-acting Texan wasn't smiling as he and his companion entered, looked steadily at the marshal as the Texan said, 'Nice town you got here, mister. Some son of a bitch raided our saddle-bags, took the extra dodgers on the woman, an' the liveryman said he was over at the café, saw no one. You know why he didn't see anyone? Because the thief come down the back alley an', accordin' to his boot tracks, he left the same way. You want to know what I think, Marshal?'

Dexter waited.

'I think whoever stole them posters had a reason.'

'And . . . ?'

'Whoever the son of a bitch was he maybe knows that woman, which means sure as I'm standin' here Art and me'll stay awhile . . . Marshal?'

'Stay as long as you like,' Dexter replied. 'Think what you want to think, but mister, let me tell you somethin': this is my territory and you don't do anythin' without tellin' me first.'

The Texan reacted to that statement, his normal amiable expression showed something different when he said, 'It's a free country, Marshal. Folks can go where they want to.'

Dexter did not dispute this when he replied to the Texan. 'I didn't say you can't go where you want to. What I said was don't do anythin' without tellin' me first.' Dexter arose, he was a tad shorter than either of the manhunters. 'Gents, you're strangers in a territory that don't take kindly to outsiders.'

The testy man's eyes flashed. 'You're threatenin' us?'

Dexter smiled, went to the door, opened it and jerked his head. Waters and Roberts left. Dexter closed the door so he didn't hear Waters tell his companion that he'd bet a new saddle they wouldn't have to do much more searching. The Texan said, 'Let's go visit the saloon,' and they crossed the road without noticing the storekeeper watching from his roadway window, turned north on the duck boards and walked as far as the saloon.

Arnie left his apron atop a counter and scurried over to the jailhouse where Marshal Dexter met him with a sour look. Buscomb said, 'They missed the dodgers?'

'Yes, an' if there was ever a chance they'd ride on, they won't now. Arnie, for . . . '

'Marshal, folks in town knows she lives on Forest Mountain. Posters or no posters, if they ask around, sooner or later, someone would tell them.'

That was true. Dexter rocked back in his chair gazing out the open door. 'I had in mind, maybe they'd leave you the dodger an' ride on . . . now I got to make that ride.'

The storekeeper hadn't thought the marshal wouldn't have to make the ride up yonder and warn the tall woman, he had thought maybe the lawman might not get up yonder in time.

Dexter heaved up out of his chair, glanced out the roadway window as the pair of manhunters emerged from the store. He said, 'Arnie, they'll want to know why you didn't put the dodger in the window.'

Buscomb came to the window, muttered something and left. Dexter watched the manhunters make the interception and follow Buscomb back into the store.

He could lock them up, but he'd need a charge and at the moment he couldn't think of one; they hadn't been in town long enough to have made an infraction.

He watched them leave the store walking north, when they were well on their way he crossed the road and Rebecca met him with a sharp remark. 'Arnie fidgeted so I told them the reason we didn't put their poster in the window was because there's a town ordinance against signs in store windows.'

Dexter looked steadily at the woman, and smiled. For a fact the business establishments on both sides of the roadway had signs over their front doors indicating what kind of business was conducted inside but had no window signs. There was indeed such an ordinance.

Arnie was mopping sweat and offered Marshal Dexter a feeble smile as he said, 'She's quicker'n I am on her feet. In my opinion those two are trouble. Mean trouble.'

His wife turned on her husband. 'I told you to put those posters back where you got them. Whether you believe it or not, Arnie, the store is our business. We got no other concern. I know the Smith woman looked after you, but that wound wouldn't have killed you anyway. Once more Arnold Buscomb, you don't go up to those mountain lakes to fish unless you take someone with you, an' don't look at me. I can't stand taking those wriggling creatures off a hook and I don't like their smell.'

Marshal Dexter left. He felt like a fifth wheel. Rebecca Buscomb hardly noticed his departure and her husband didn't either; he was occupied trying to counter her tongue lashing.

Dexter went down to the livery barn. The day man showed him the strangers horses. Later, Dexter went up to the saloon where the barman told him the strangers had been there but that had been more than an hour earlier.

Dexter stood out front of the saloon. Winchester was not a large place, it was somewhere between a village and a town. He could not imagine the manhunters visiting the old gnome who wore celluloid collars at his apothecary store, nor the harness works or the other business concerns, and certainly not the church. That left the eatery. He walked down there, pushed in and of a half-dozen diners who didn't look around when he entered, two did look around — Art Waters and Will Roberts. They were having a midday meal. None of the three men nodded. Dexter sat at the counter and nodded for a cup of java as he told the caféman he didn't want anything else, and the caféman's thick eyebrows climbed upwards like a pair of caterpillars but he said nothing, he had other customers.

6

A Reason for Worry

When the unpleasant bounty hunter finished eating and arose, his partner lingered to drain his coffee cup.

Art Waters came up where the lawman was sitting and said, 'We can make this easy, Marshal. We'll split the bounty three ways, a third to you?'

Dexter arose ignoring Waters and facing Roberts. 'That's mighty generous. Have you found her?'

Roberts avoided a direct answer. 'I don't expect that'll be too hard.' He paused. 'You was right, Winchester ain't a friendly town to strangers.'

'Mister Roberts, I expect most towns don't like havin' bounty hunters ride in.'

'The bounty is eight hunnert dollars,'

Roberts said, and at the widened gaze of the marshal, he also said, 'Mister Ames is a rich man. You want one-third?'

The burly, balding blacksmith came in booming a greeting to the marshal and the caféman. It was a welcome interruption. The manhunters looked stonily at the blacksmith, then left the café.

The blacksmith stared at Dexter. 'I didn't mean to butt in. I got their animals at the smithy for new shoes.' The blacksmith paused to consider the frowning caféman behind his counter. He shook his head and said it again, 'I didn't mean to butt in,' and went to the counter to sit as Marshal Dexter left the eatery.

Across the road, he went into the cell room and brought the prisoner to his office, sat him on a bench across from the desk and asked him a pointed question.

'How much bounty is on you for shooting the whip?'

'It wasn't the whip, it was the gun guard, an' I got no idea if there's a reward on me or not. I got the hell away as fast as I could.'

'How much did you get from the robbery?'

Coyle's gaze swivelled away then back. He was not an accomplished liar. 'Not much, some trinkets off the passengers is about all.'

'No money? No mail pouches?'

The outlaw showed disdain when he said, 'I didn't take the mail pouches. Just some money.' He paused. 'Mail pouches don't usually have no cash, just letters, an' I had a friend who took pouches an' the sky fell on him. There was US marshals on his trail like a pack of wolves. They run him down. I never took mail pouches.'

'How much money did you get?'

Coyle's tongue made a swift circuit of his lips before he replied. 'Three hunnert dollars.'

'That's all?'

'I'm not lyin' to you. Three hunnert,

some gold rings an' a drummer's diamond stick pin.'

Dexter leaned on his desk. 'There's a pair of bounty hunters in town. Fellers named Roberts and Waters.'

The outlaw's colour faded, his close-spaced eyes rapidly moved. He licked his lips again. 'There's the law business, Marshal. They can't just ride into another state or territory an' take someone.'

Dexter nodded and faintly smiled. 'Tell them that, Luther.'

For a long moment the outlaw was silent. It did not help his anxiety that the lawman across from him was still wearing that humourless small smile. Eventually he said, 'How much reward on me?'

Dexter avoided a direct answer. 'For murder, Luther, it's usually enough to interest bounty hunters.'

For a long moment the lawman was quiet. He leaned back off the desk, drifted his gaze to the wall rack of weapons, to the little barred roadway window and back as he finally spoke.

'They'll be along directly.'

The outlaw straightened up on the bench. 'I'll double the reward, Marshal.'

Dexter snorted. 'You wouldn't have that kind of money.'

'I got a cache up north.'

'They all have a cache, Luther. I've had that offer made a dozen times.' Dexter leaned forward on the desk, hands clasped. 'When you came south where was you headin'?'

'Messico. A friend I knew went down there. He tol' me when he come back after a couple of years US lawmen can't go down there on a trail.'

'The storekeeper's big old mare wouldn't have got you that far.'

'I figured to use her until I could find somethin' better.'

'Luther, I don't think three hundred dollars would keep you goin' for long down yonder.'

'Well . . . maybe I could hire out

along the way. I was a top hand once.'

'Maybe, an' the first time you told someone about the woman up yonder on Forest Mountain folks'd start askin' how you know an' other questions. They'd want to know why you didn't try'n collect bounty on her.'

Luther Coyle's eyes did not waver this time when he spoke. 'That damned female woman is a jinx on me. But for her I wouldn't be settin' here with bounty hunters lookin' for me. I wish to Chris' I'd never seen her, or that storekeeper, or his big old stud-necked mare!'

Dexter returned the prisoner to his cell. Coyle complained about being hungry and the marshal said he'd take care of that, locked up from out front and went over to the eatery and got a surprise: the pair of bounty hunters were drinking coffee at the counter. They barely looked up and did not nod. Marshal Dexter ignored them, told the caféman he wanted a pail of stew and a pail of black coffee.

The caféman brought the little pails, did not say a word and watched Marshal Dexter cross in the direction of the jailhouse.

One of the bounty hunters spoke. 'Friend, who's he got locked up over there?'

The caféman gave a short answer. 'I mind my business an' he minds his business. I don't ask questions. You gents need more coffee?'

They didn't. They arose, trickled silver beside the empty cups and returned to the doorway to roll and light cigarettes.

Waters said, 'He wouldn't have the woman over there, would he?'

The raffish Texan's reply was non-committal. 'I got no idea. Why would he have?'

Waters' answer was slowly given. 'I got a feelin' that it ain't so much these folks not likin' strangers as it's some notion they got not to say anythin' 'bout Catbird Ames, or whatever name she's using.'

'You think we found her?' asked the Texan.

'Not exactly, but of all the places we been searchin' this here place is the first one that's sure as hell hidin' somethin' an' my guess is that it's her. Let's go have another talk with the law.'

Lex Dexter was cleaning rifles and carbines plus two sawn-off shotguns from the wall rack when the manhunters entered. They exchanged nods and the Texan considered a short-barrelled scattergun the marshal had been cleaning as he said, 'That barrel's shorter'n most, ain't it? A man standin' in a doorway could clear a roadway without moving if he used that thing.'

They cryptic bounty hunter allowed no time for Dexter to answer when he said, 'You got a prisoner, Marshal?'

'Yes, I got one. Why?'

'Male or female?'

Dexter wiped oily hands before replying, 'Male.'

The unpleasant man continued his questions. 'What'd he do?'

'Stopped a coach up north an' shot the gun guard.'

Over an interlude of silence the bounty hunters exchanged a look before the unpleasant man said, 'What's his name?'

Dexter was reloading the scattergun and snapped it closed before speaking again. 'You got a lot of questions, mister. Now it's my turn. That woman you're after, she shot her husband?'

'Murdered him in cold blood, Marshal.'

'Why?'

'Hell, I don't know. My job's to find her an' haul her back.'

'So his father can buy off a judge an' get her hung?'

The unpleasant man's eyes narrowed on Dexter. 'Our job's to find her, mister, that's all.' Waters paused without blinking or changing expression. 'Are you a judge?'

Dexter returned the other man's stare without blinking and ignored the question when he said, 'You been askin' questions around town?' and the unpleasant man nodded slightly. 'That's part of our job.'

'Did you find out anythin'?'

Art Waters gave one of his cryptic responses. 'My job ain't to give information, Marshal, it's to get it.' After a pause Waters also said, 'That prisoner you got, is his name Luther Coyle?'

'He told me it's Barney Noble.'

Waters barely inclined his head. 'That'll be Luther. He used the name Barney Noble at a hotel where he stayed a spell up where he stopped the stage.'

For the first time the Texan spoke, he said, 'He's a penny-ante son of a bitch. Steals cattle'n horses, robs old folks in their homes, an' stops stages when he figures it's safe. The last time he shot the gun guard. Hit him between the inside of his left arm an' his ribs. When he fell off the coach' Coyle robbed his pockets. The guard's name is Rafe Fortier. He told us when he's feelin' better he's going to track Coyle to the end of the earth if he has to an' blow his head off. An' Marshal, we know Rafe Fortier, when he says somethin' he does it.'

Dexter put the scattergun on his desk and spoke as he was straightening up. 'What's he worth, gents?'

Will Roberts answered in his curt manner. 'A hunnert dollars. If he'd killed Rafe it would have been more. Marshal, we'd like to take him back with the woman.' Roberts paused. 'You'd get one third for him too.'

Dexter was tiring of this. 'You got to have extradition papers. From your governor making the request an' from the office of our governor agreeing.'

The Texan was disgusted. 'You know how long all that takes? Just hand 'em over to us an' when we get up north an' collect on 'em we'll send you your share.'

Dexter returned the shotgun to its rack and while pulling through the chain and locking it he replied to the

Texan. 'Can't do that,' he said, and returned to stand behind his desk.

The unpleasant manhunter jerked his head and the pair left the jailhouse. They went up to the saloon, got a bottle, two jolt glasses and took them to a table. Art Waters was less curt and more antagonistic when he spoke while filling the small glasses. 'Sure as we're settin' here there's somethin' goin' on.' He paused to down his whiskey, pushed the empty glass aside and fixed his companion with a hard look. 'Will, they wouldn't have no reason to steal the dodgers an' act about half hostile unless they had a reason.'

'An' you figure they know somethin' about the Ames woman?'

Waters refilled his glass but did not lift it as he spoke softly. 'That lawman's hostile. To me, I'd say it's not because we're strangers nor bounty men, it's because he's got a personal reason. I've run into 'em before that won't cooperate . . . Tell you what; you stay in town and watch the marshal. I'm goin' to ride out, maybe find some rangemen or a ranch headquarters where they might know about the woman.'

The Texan refilled his glass wearing a frown. 'What would rangemen know?'

'That's what I figure to find out. I'll be back come supper-time.'

The residents of Winchester were beginning to understand why the strangers were in town and, even among those who knew little or nothing about the tall woman, there was a common dislike of bounty hunters.

The Texan was unctuous by nature otherwise he couldn't have continued to partner up with the unpleasant man, but unctuousness was irritating. While he slouched in different places watching the jailhouse he met people and asked questions. The answers he got were either glaring silence or declarations of innocence of ever even having heard of the tall woman.

Some of this got back to Marshal

Dexter and, while he was satisfied, he had no illusions; sooner or later, especially if cash was offered, someone would tell him about the tall woman.

It was Arnie Buscomb and Fred Muller, the blacksmith, who came to the jailhouse to say that one of the strangers had left town riding west and the other one was watching the jailhouse from doorways and dog trots. Marshal Dexter thanked them. After their departure he was glad it wasn't the other way around. He had a low opinion of the Texan but the unpleasant manhunter worried him.

Later, with the day ending, he visited the livery barn to ask questions about the stranger riding out alone. The liveryman said, 'He ain't a likable feller. He went due west, Marshal. That's all I can tell you. If you want, when he comes back I'll let you know.'

Dexter nodded about that and went to the eatery for an early supper. He was the only customer who provided the caféman with an opportunity to start a conversation. Dexter wasn't in the mood for this so the caféman let his one-sided discussion dwindle. During the interlude of silence between them, the Texan walked in, sat down and smiled at both the caféman and the marshal. He ordered and leaned back off the counter to address the lawman.

'This here's good stock country?'

Dexter nodded without speaking.

The Texan tried again. 'Me'n Art been at this business five, six years. Mostly we do right good. A few times . . . mostly because the fellers we're after get below the border before we can catch 'em.'

Again the marshal nodded without looking up. When the caféman brought the Texan's supper, he glared and his angry expression kept the Texan from trying to strike up another conversation.

As the marshal arose to leave he addressed the Texan. 'Your partner's been gone a long time.'

The Texan had to swivel on the bench to see the lawman who was at the roadway door. 'He likes this country, Marshal. Mostly, places we've had to go he didn't like, but he likes this country even if the folks aren't real friendly.'

Dexter nodded, closed the door after himself, gazed northerly where dusk was shadowing distances, and went up to the livery barn, rigged out his horse and rode up the back alley as far north as the end of town, then set his animal into a rocking-chair lope and held him to it for two miles.

He saw no other rider. In fact he didn't even see cattle until he was able to make out Forest Mountain with dusk fast fading into evening.

His idea to elude the Texan's clumsy spying had worked. By the time he dropped from a lope to a walk neither he nor his horse were visible from Winchester.

The Texan didn't worry him but his partner did. Very probably the Texan would not look very hard for the vanished lawman but his companion, Art Waters would. He would find that the lawman's horse was missing.

What Roberts might do was anyone's guess but he would be unable to track the marshal in darkness. Still, Dexter did not underestimate the man.

He was part way up the trail to Caitlin Rourke's meadow when he halted to look back and listen. He heard a cow bawling but that was all. He continued to the meadow and halted again with a bad feeling. No light showed. He swung down, led his horse to the corral to loop the reins, did not see the mare or colt and blew out a long breath. The clearing had an air of desertion.

He went to the cabin and rattled the door twice. There was no response until he raised his fist to knock a third time and an unmistakable female voice spoke from the north corner of the cabin.

'Drop your gun and face around!'

Dexter let the six-gun fall, turned, and said, 'Lex Dexter.'

She remained in shadowy darkness. 'What do you want? I'm not going with . . .'

'I want to talk. Just talk.'

She appeared soundlessly with the carbine tilted, her finger inside the trigger guard and halted where they could see each other. She said, 'Talk.'

He obeyed. 'There's a pair of bounty hunters in town looking for you. They was sent by your father-in-law up north. He put a healthy bounty on you.'

She grounded the Winchester, moved a little closer and spoke quietly. 'I'm packed. I'll be gone come daylight.'

'Where's the mare?'

'Behind the shed where she can't be seen. I've been expecting someone. I heard you coming up the trail.'

He said, 'They'll find you. So far they haven't learned much or they'd have been up here, but they figure you're hereabouts. I told them they couldn't take you back without signed extradition orders. It's the law for a fact, but I needed time.'

She edged past, opened the door, led the way inside and asked him in the dark if he thought it would be safe to light a candle.

He said, 'It's likely safe, all the same don't do it. They know by now I left town but I didn't tell anyone where I was goin' an' they can't read sign until sunup.'

She sat on a bench at the table, leaned the Winchester aside and regarded him. 'You're taking a chance, Marshal. Why?'

He sat on the same bench, thumbed back his hat and made a rueful small smile she could barely discern. 'Maybe you wouldn't understand. I've been a lawman for some time. Long enough to be satisfied that sometimes there's no connection between book law and justice. If those manhunters got you . . . it's a long lonely ride back up yonder. They'd collect the bounty when they got back whether you was sitting your saddle or was tied belly down across it.'

His eyes had made enough adaptation to enable him to see her face well enough. She looked ten years younger. 'Would you like some coffee?' she asked and he declined; the scent of wood smoke carried great distances.

She held both hands clasped in her lap in silence until he said, 'Except for Barney Noble, or whatever his name is, you might be fairly safe. Folks in town know you an' they don't like strangers. By now they know who the strangers are an' bounty hunters aren't liked most places I've been.'

'I hate to leave, Marshal. I love this place. It's home to me'n my mare, and her baby.' She looked straight at him. 'But I have to. Like you said, they'll find me up here.'

He pushed out his legs and leaned back with both elbows atop the table. 'I've done some figurin'. Whether things pan out or not don't leave until you see two rough-lookin' strangers comin' up your trail.'

He could tell that hadn't been a reassuring remark so he added to it. 'I'll warn you.' He met her gaze and smiled straight at her. 'You got friends in Winchester. The storekeeper did a stupid thing: he stole the Wanted dodgers on you from the saddle-bags of one of those strangers, and that was the same as tellin' them you might be hereabouts. He meant well. Arnie's a good man. He'll never forget what he owes you . . . Caitlin, it's a long ride back.' He stood up and reset his hat. She remained on the bench watching him. When she finally arose she said, 'I know better'n to ask personal questions, but . . . '

'Fire away, ma'am.'

'Why aren't you married?'

He got as far as the doorway before answering. 'I just never got around to it.' They went out where his horse was dozing. As he unlooped the reins and thumbed the cinch he said, 'Watch for two strangers, otherwise stay close.

You've got friends.'

She watched him head back in the direction of the trail.

When she could no longer see or hear him she went behind the shed, brought the mare and colt out front, forked them two separate piles of meadow hay and went to sit on the nearby stump and listen to the mare eat. The colt was a tad young but it nosed the hay anyway.

Somewhere northward where Forest Mountain rose steadily to its timbered crest, a wolf sounded. There was no answer for an excellent reason, the mating season was past.

7

A Wildly Desperate Idea

Dexter wasn't surprised the morning after his night ride to Forest Mountain when the Texan walked into the jailhouse trailed by his unsmiling partner.

Dexter spoke first; he asked how the unpleasant man's ride had been and got a surly answer. 'Stockmen aroun' here ain't very neighbourly. I never got a direct answer from any of 'em.'

Dexter smiled. 'It's nice to be liked isn't it?'

The unpleasant man considered the lawman coldly. 'You have a nice ride last night?'

'It's cooler at night. Somethin' I can do for you?'

'Where is she?'

'Who?'

Waters glowered. 'Marshal, I made

you a decent offer: one third of both bounties. This is the last time I say that.'

Dexter nodded and waited.

Waters' face reddened. 'We're goin' up north where there's a telegraph and get Mister Ames to send a US Marshal down here.'

Dexter wasn't smiling when he answered. 'Mister, a killin' that don't break federal law . . . '

The Texan piped in, 'You don't know Mister Ames. In our part of the country when he says jump even the law jumps.' Roberts paused, clearly angry. 'You never said where you rode out last night.'

Dexter hesitated briefly before going to the door and opening it. 'Out!'

As he was closing the door after Waters and the Texan, the unpleasant man turned and said, 'Mister, you just bit off more'n you can chew.'

Dexter closed the door. He was still upset a half-hour later when Arnie Buscomb came over from the store to expound on an idea he and his wife had devised.

'We could adopt her, make her our daughter.'

Dexter considered the older man. 'Arnie, if her safety depended on havin' folks, it'd be a good idea, but the way things stand it wouldn't help.'

The storekeeper went to a bench and sat down, his expression showing exasperation. Dexter dropped down at his desk opposite the storekeeper at the moment Arnie Buscomb pointedly said, 'Marshal, we got to get rid of those bounty hunters.'

Dexter couldn't disagree with that.

'The blacksmith an' his helper could work them men over until they'd wish they'd never been born.'

Dexter leaned back from his desk. 'She'd sure appreciate you takin' her side so much, but cripplin' up those bounty men would most likely get the feller who hired them to send down others. Maybe five or six others.'

The storekeeper threw up his hands

and left the bench. 'Marshal, you knock 'em down as fast as I set 'em up. Now that you've told me what not to do, tell me what I can do.'

'I'm doin' some figurin',' the lawman replied 'If it comes to needin' help I'll look you up.'

After the storekeeper had departed, Marshal Dexter rolled his eyes heavenward and gave his head a slight wag.

His prisoner was dragging a tin cup across the cell bars and yelling to be fed. Dexter ignored the racket. Part of his idea had gelled. Luther Coyle believed the manhunters were seeking him, which is what the lawman wanted him to think. He had reason for wanting Coyle to be scairt peeless.

He also had reason not to tell Luther that he wasn't wanted for murder, he hadn't killed that gun guard.

He considered Luther more an annoyance than a problem. It did no good to wish the outlaw hadn't heard what Caitlin Rourke had said about being a fugitive. But that too was water under the bridge. Luther *did* know and because he'd been born with a tongue that hinged in the middle and flapped at both ends he had to be kept caged and away from people. He had already mentioned a little of what he knew and while Dexter thought he hadn't been believed that was something he wouldn't want to wager a lead penny on.

The liveryman came up to the jailhouse to say, 'Them strangers rode out goin' north. I figured you might want to know.'

After the liveryman's departure Marshal Dexter swore. It was probably inevitable that they had learned about the whereabouts of the tall woman but that did not make him feel any better.

He crossed the road to ask Arnie Buscomb to look after his prisoner, went down to the livery barn for his animal and without a word to anyone left Winchester by the west side alley travelling north.

A couple of miles out he saw a pair of horsemen riding in the direction of Forest Mountain. If he'd had doubts before he had none now. *Waters and the Texan knew!*

It was still early in the day but with a long ride ahead it could be expected that shadows would be forming about the time he started up the tall woman's trail. Also, with as long a lead as the bounty hunters had they would arrive at her clearing before Dexter could.

His objective was overtaking the manhunters. That was all he thought about until he could make out the upward trail with the sun getting lower. Not until he was going up the trail did he think about his purpose in relation to his lawman's oath.

A horse whinnied shortly before he came out of the trees into the clearing. He stopped, dismounted and led his animal to the final tier of standing pines and firs.

There was no sign of the bounty hunters or their horses. Neither was there any sign of Caitlin Rourke although her mare and colt were in the corral. He watched them for signs of concern or curiosity. The mare was ripping up stalks of feed, her colt was nosing along the corral stringers. Neither animal showed signs of interest in anything except their individual preoccupations.

Dexter retraced his steps, left his mount tethered and returned to the clearing's edge to stand motionless while blocking in particular areas of study.

The mare, the house, the clearing with treetop birds, even the little creek were as natural and seemingly undisturbed as they could be.

The marshal circled north-westerly among the trees seeking tracks, boot tracks or shod-horse tracks and found nothing. It was almost eerie. The bounty hunters had come up the trail ahead of him, he had seen their sign. While it was possible the tall woman had gone searching for small game, he found no tracks to substantiate this possibility.

He had only circled in one direction, north-westerly. He returned to his horse, which was dozing, hiked past eastward, again staying invisible among huge old trees and came across fresh scuff where horses had left their mark.

The bounty men hadn't entered the clearing. Dexter nodded about this. Waters and the Texan were old hands at manhunting. In this case they hadn't taken chances by appearing in the clearing.

Now, he worried. No sign of Caitlin was particularly unsettling. Roberts and Waters were as capable as Indians, they could read sign and approach the tall woman from behind, if she were in the westerly timber. Dexter saw no sign of that, only the tracks of a pair of shod horses, which he followed with caution.

He paused often to listen. Shod horses made sounds especially over hard ground — called *caliche* — but spongy layers of ancient pine and fir needles muted noise.

As he tracked he speculated on how far the manhunters were ahead on the trail, how much time had elapsed, and arrived at the conclusion that unless they stopped it would be close to dusk before he saw them.

It was a fair surmise. He had crossed a creek where muddy water indicated animals had tanked up and was shouldering his way out of the customary creek willows when he heard crows. When he saw them they were winging easterly and making raucous noises as they went.

Something had disturbed them. Marshal Dexter fixed the direction from which they had come and altered his course as he left the creek.

For a tracker, the endless forest gloom was an ally as were the crushed needles where shod animals had passed. He was less cautious for an excellent reason, he wanted to find the manhunters before sundown.

He encountered an indication that the Texan and his companion were not travelling alone. Where they abruptly turned northerly he found a blue bandanna that smelled faintly of something pleasant like pine soap.

They had her!

He was tempted to go back for his horse. If he did so, by the time he got back in the vicinity of the creek it would be too dark to track.

He pocketed the handkerchief and increased his pace. The second creek was fed by a waterfall. He heard the water before he saw the creek and the clearing it traversed.

Two saddle horses were hobbled in tall grass. Dexter did not have to discern the dark sweat stains on their backs to be satisfied. He blended in speckled shadows for a long time waiting for the people to appear. When they did not for a considerable length of time but did eventually appear the marshal briefly held his breath. Caitlin limped, her appearance was of demoralized resignation.

The men behind her growled when she should stop. They rummaged oversized saddle-bags for the means of a meal and told Caitlin to sit on the ground and not to move.

Dexter could hear everything that was said. He waited until the men were sitting and eating then began a careful hike northerly to get behind them. The Texan tossed Caitlin a scrap of food. His unpleasant companion ignored the tall woman.

Dexter was making good progress until he encountered a boulder field of stones almost as large as a house. He had to go far upcountry to get around them and when he came back to lower country the bounty hunters had finished their meal and the unpleasant man was smoking. The Texan had a cud tucked into his cheek.

The Texan worked at getting a conversation going with the tall woman. Dexter could hear every word. The unpleasant bounty hunter ignored them both to wander out to look at their animals.

Dexter was sidling southward using forest gloom as an ally when the Texan said, 'Ma'am, he talks rough but he really ain't. I've known him some years.'

Caitlin's reply was short. 'It's a long ride back up north.'

The Texan spat then smiled. 'Ma'am, we've brung 'em back from a lot further.'

Caitlin made a shrewd observation. 'You can't make good time in this mountainous country with two of us on one horse.'

The Texan had an answer to that too. 'Only until we find another animal. Until then we'll favour my horse. It'll take time but, ma'am, that's one thing me'n Art got lots of.'

Dexter's interest was in the man called Art Waters; he needed both manhunters together not separated. While waiting, he edged closer to the clearing. When he finally halted within handgun range he heard the Texan say, 'Lady, Mister Ames ain't exactly a forgivin' feller.'

Caitlin's response was curt. 'There's nothing you can tell me about him that I don't know.'

'Well,' responded the Texan, 'we got a long ride, plenty of time to do some ponderin', but right now I'm wonderin' how much you'd pay to be set loose.'

Dexter watched the unpleasant man returning from the horses. Of the two bounty hunters he considered the one named Art Waters to be the most dangerous.

When the unpleasant man got back among the horse gear and squatted looking at Caitlin, the Texan told him he had mentioned making some kind of trade instead of taking her all the way back.

Waters was silent as long as he was required to vigorously scratch, then he ignored Caitlin to growl at his partner, 'She ain't got nothin'. This one can't buy her way out.'

The Texan looked at the tall woman. 'Is that right, ma'am?'

She avoided a direct reply when she said, 'My guess is that you're businessmen.' Before either manhunter could ask what that meant she also said, 'Milk me dry if you can and take me up north for the bounty. Get paid both ways . . . except that all I own is back in that clearing where I live.'

Waters put a sour look on the Texan, 'I could've told you so.'

The Texan was not entirely crestfallen. In a defensive tone he said, 'It's worked other times, Art,' and this time did not even get a withering look.

Dexter was motionless in the last tier of forest mammoths. Daylight was fading, not rapidly but inevitably when he raised his six-gun and spoke not loudly because if he could hear them they could hear him.

He said, 'Toss the guns away an' set still. Don't move. *Do it!*'

The surprised bounty hunters were shocked into temporary speechlessness.

Dexter repeated the order, louder the second time. When the manhunters remained motionless Caitlin Rourke arose, went behind each man, emptied their holsters and stood erect peering in the direction of the man whose voice she had recognized.

Dexter moved clear of the trees. The bounty hunters regarded him from faces set in stone.

Caitlin spoke quietly. 'I was out gathering berries. I didn't even hear them.'

Dexter dryly said, 'Ma'am, you got to get a dog,' as he came closer.

The Texan, true to his nature, spoke in an almost whining tone of voice. 'Marshal, we're just doin' what we was hired to do. We didn't break no laws. We . . .'

The unpleasant man said, 'Shut up!'

The Texan closed his mouth. Caitlin smiled at Dexter when he came up. He couldn't recall seeing her smile before. He had a decision to make; they wouldn't make it out of the forest into open country before nightfall and herding two prisoners through ranks of huge trees in darkness would guarantee he wouldn't arrive in town with any prisoners.

The unpleasant man, wearing a bitter expression, finally spoke. He and his companion had come a long way. They had found their victim and faced an equally long return trip. He asked if the marshal had come alone and when Dexter nodded, Waters dryly said, 'Mister, when we don't get back, Mister Ames'll send others an' when they know we stopped huntin' for her here, they'll figure out why.'

Dexter leathered his handgun and squatted. 'So you got some idea? Shoot.'

'Give us Luther Coyle, three hunnert dollars an' we'll tell Mister Ames the woman was kicked in the head by a horse an' is buried down here.'

Dexter and Caitlin exchanged a glance. It was possible they were both marvelling at the calm and easy way the unpleasant man had a solution to everything. It probably impressed Caitlin more than it did the marshal; he had been handling men like Art Waters and worse for a long time.

Waters was waiting for an answer when the Texan broke the silence. 'Marshal, you got a cougar by the tail. Mister Ames ain't just rich, he's mean. He'll believe Art that the woman got horse-kicked. We'll take back some of her personal things.'

This time Caitlin rolled her eyes skyward. Dexter noticed but said nothing. He was not looking forward to a dark night in the uplands with two prisoners one of whom was as slippery as a snake.

He was hungry but that also was of no immediate concern. He handed Caitlin his six-gun, told her to shoot the first one that tried to jump her and went after his horse. It was a long hike and the darkness settled in the highlands an hour or so before it darkened open country.

Finding the horse was not difficult although being unable to read his own tracks he had to double back twice before the animal nickered. It was both hungry and thirsty.

On the ride back he was unable to find an alternative to spending the night in the clearing. He would truss both bounty hunters and sleep with one eye open.

When he was approaching the clearing he saw a feeble reflection of firelight among the darkly majestic trees, and dismounted to lead his horse close enough for the outlines of three people to be discernible.

He'd had misgivings about leaving the tall woman guarding the bounty hunters but from what he could see Waters and Roberts were sitting on the ground about where he'd left them and Caitlin was opposite them across the little fire with the gun.

He led his horse into the clearing, hobbled it, dumped the bridle, blanket and saddle, waited to see if there would be a horse fight and when it was clear his horse was only interested in eating, he hiked in the direction of the fire.

When he was close, Caitlin addressed the Texan. 'You owe me a cartwheel,' she said, and while the raffish individual made no attempt to reach into a pocket he said, 'It was a fifty-fifty bet. Some folks would've just kept on ridin'.'

Caitlin mentioned food in the saddle-bags, handed Dexter the pistol and went rummaging. While she was occupied, the unpleasant man said, 'Marshal, Mister Ames'll believe she's dead. Give up Coyle to take back an' some of her personal things.'

Dexter squatted, scratched beard stubble and shook his head. 'Luther knows things about her. You'd have a hard time makin' the feller that hired you believe she's dead. Not with Luther runnin' off at the mouth.'

The unpleasant man said no more. He and his companion concentrated on watching Caitlin make a meal without cooking utensils. Whether they were impressed or not the marshal certainly was. Once, when their eyes met Dexter wagged his head and Caitlin smiled at him.

The meal was adequate to blunt hunger otherwise it left something to be wished for, and after they had eaten Caitlin told Marshal Dexter that was the last of the food.

He used belts to bind their legs at the ankles and secure their hands behind their backs. The Texan whined. 'A man cain't sleep like this, Marshal.'

Dexter took Caitlin out a distance in the direction of their grazing animals. There was a moon, tipped up at both ends which folks said signified rain and 'folks' were wrong about this sort of thing more often than they were right.

She had a question for him which he could not answer. She said, 'What are you going to do with them?'

'They aren't outlaws as far as I know so I can't lock 'em up. I got to send them back but you stay here, an' that'll stir up more trouble because they know

I have Luther. They want to take him back too an' you know Luther, the first chance he gets he'll tell the man who sent the bounty hunters you're alive.'

Her reply was short. 'The Texan said they'd settle for Luther an' three hundred dollars. I don't have three hundred dollars but I do have five jars of placer nuggets I've sluiced from mountain creeks. My guess is that in money the gold would fetch six or maybe eight hundred dollars.'

He was impressed. He was also thoughtful. 'An' Luther'll tell your daddy-in-law what he knows.'

She hesitated long enough to glance back where only faint coals showed before saying, 'You heard the other one say if you'd give them Luther an' three hundred dollars they'd leave.'

Dexter nodded wryly. In his opinion those two would sell their mothers for money. She cut across his thoughts. 'He said he'd tell Carl Ames I got killed by a horse kick.'

This time Dexter's response was

harsh. 'If they were believed, Mister Ames would likely pay them for their hunt an' the law'd settle for Luther. Caitlin, there's one problem: Luther's got to believe you got killed.'

She had an answer. 'For all five jars of gold they'd likely tell Carl Ames they saw me dead on the ground.'

The marshal looked skyward, in the direction of the dying coals and finally at the tall woman, and grinned. 'You're as sly as a 'coon in a hen house.'

She smiled at him. 'Take the mean one aside . . . '

'His name is Waters.'

'Take Waters aside, give him the proposition an', if he agrees, in the morning when we go back to my clearing I'll manage to get kicked.'

'How?'

'My mare won't let anyone, not even me, get between her an' her colt.'

Dexter looked sceptical. She saw his expression and spoke again, 'Leave it to me, Marshal. After I get kicked you crawl into the corral, lift my head an' say my neck's broke.'

He regarded her again, this time without shaking his head. 'Let's go back, Caitlin. If this works I'm a bear with a sore behind.'

As he turned she shyly felt for his hand and gripped it. He returned the squeeze.

Shortly before they were within earshot of the camp he said, 'If the mare kicks you . . . Folks get horse-kicked every day an' some die, an' Waters is not a fool.'

She said nothing.

8

A Dangerous Plan

The bounty hunters were understandably uncomfortable. The unpleasant one glared in stoic silence but his companion, the Texan, didn't. While Caitlin was out gathering dead wood for the fire Will Roberts whined and swore.

Marshal Dexter was stoking the fire with twigs when the unpleasant man said, 'Do you know what you're doin' Marshal? You're makin' prisoners of two fellers that haven't broke no law, an' that, in case you didn't know it, is a violation of the law. You can't keep prisoners without charges.'

Dexter considered the rumpled, filthy and unshaven manhunter. 'Are you savvy about the law, Mister Roberts?'

'Savvy enough, Marshal. I was a lawman over in Idaho for three years.'

Dexter accepted that. 'But bounty hunting pays better?'

'A lot better; an' you're takin' sides with a murderer, an' holdin' us hostage. Mister Ames won't like any of this.'

Caitlin returned with an armload of deadfalls which she dumped as the unpleasant man made another statement. 'When Mister Ames gets through pullin' rank with the governor an' others, you won't be able to get another lawman job as long as you live.'

When the fire was blazing, Marshal Dexter approached the unpleasant man without a word, untied him, hauled him up to his feet and jabbed him from behind in the direction of the distant horses.

Waters only spoke once. 'If you shoot me, mister, it'll be the biggest mistake you ever made.'

When they were out where the marshal and the tall woman had been, the lawman said, 'Sit down. Not a word, just set and listen.'

Waters obeyed. He had to look up because Dexter remained standing when he began speaking. Waters listened. At first his expression was sceptical but the longer Dexter spoke the more the unpleasant man's expression changed. When Dexter had said all he intended to say, the bounty hunter leaned to pluck a stalk of grass to chew on as he considered the lawman in long silence. Eventually he said, 'How much gold's in them jars?'

Dexter had no idea. 'I'd guess more'n three hundred dollars' worth. Waters, Ames will pay you, you can have Luther Coyle and the gold.'

'Mister, it won't wash. I'd be in favour except for the woman. Mister Ames . . . '

'She'll be dead. Her mare kicked her an' broke her neck. She'll be dead and buried with a head-board in place before you get home.'

Waters spat out the grass stalk and stared. 'Dead . . . ?'

'You can look at the corpse. When

146

you get back you can say you saw the body.'

Water's gaze shifted, he unwound up off the ground. 'You're goin' to kill her?'

Dexter sounded exasperated when he replied, 'No one's goin' to get killed but you'll tell Mister Ames how she died.'

'What about Luther Coyle?'

'He'll take the word of you'n the Texan she's dead. You both saw her dead.'

Waters plucked another grass stalk but this time he did not raise it, he twisted it with his fingers. 'Will?'

'He'll see the corpse too an' you can tell him the mare kicked and busted her neck.' Dexter paused. 'Your Texan can verify it when you tell Mister Ames she is dead.'

The bounty hunter had the expression of someone who had swallowed a quince. He did not look at the town marshal when eventually he said, 'You sure about that gold?'

147

'I'm sure.'

Waters dropped the stalk of grass and looked straight at the marshal. 'One thing, Marshal, don't say anythin' to my partner about this. We work well enough together but he's like a parrot, he tells anythin' he knows.'

Dexter agreed. 'He won't know any more'n he's supposed to know.'

Again the unpleasant man hung fire before speaking. 'When we leave here we go back to the woman's cabin?'

'Yes.'

'Will's goin' to wonder why we don't go straight down to your town.'

Dexter shrugged. 'That's up to you. I expect he'll believe any lie you make up.'

'Where'd she get that gold?'

Dexter ignored the question to say, 'It's a long ride. You want to take my offer or not?'

As before the manhunter hesitated. This wasn't the first time a fugitive had tried to bargain with him but at least this time he would make money at both ends. He twisted to look back where the tall woman and his partner was sitting. When he faced back he said, 'It's chancy, Marshal.'

Dexter agreed, it was indeed chancy.

Art Waters abruptly inclined his head as he said, 'When do I get the gold?'

'When we get back to the cabin.'

Water's mind was made up. As he turned in the direction of the camp he said, 'Let's get to ridin'.'

When they returned where the others had waited Waters told the Texan to go bring in their horses and stood watching until his partner was well out of hearing before he looked at Caitlin and asked if she knew what the marshal had told him out yonder.

She nodded without arising from the ground.

Waters asked another question, 'Is that nugget gold?'

This time she stood up when she answered. 'It's nuggets, some are fair size but mostly they're small. Five bottles of them.'

'What would you say they might fetch in money?'

'I'd guess somewhere between six an' eight hundred dollars.'

Waters looked at the marshal who was busy picking nettles off his trousers. He looked back at the tall woman. 'Don't try nothin'. The marshal an' me've made a trade.'

Caitlin looked long at Lex Dexter then scooped up a bridle and went to meet Roberts.

Waters stood watching her cross toward the Texan and made a mild remark. 'Marshal, a woman like that'd make a man quit eatin' snuff.'

Evidently the unctuous Texan thought so because as they were returning with the horses he said, 'Ma'am, did you ever figure to marry?'

She was startled and showed it. 'You'd have to take an all-over bath, get shorn an' shaved, mister, an' some woman might want you but I sure wouldn't.'

The Texan was daunted. 'I've seen

150

how you look at the town marshal.'

Caitlin lengthened her stride. The bounty hunter had to scurry to keep up. When they reached Dexter and the unpleasant man she said, 'Marshal, would you mind if I rode double with you?'

It was doubtful if the Texan understood the rebuff. In any event he would have had no time to sulk. Art Waters said, 'Saddle up.' The marshal told Waters and Roberts to ride double.

It was a quiet party that rode across the little meadow in the direction of the tall woman's clearing.

What eventually brought their attention was a horse whinnying. The bounty hunters were inclined to stop but Caitlin was in the lead and didn't even pause. She knew that sound.

The sun was sifting through tree tops where it could when they came to the tall woman's clearing. The mare whinnied again and her owner ignored the men to ride directly to the corral.

Without looking around she climbed into the corral, forked a mound of cured grass to the mare and stood leaning on the fork handle watching the colt lip up several bits of hay and spit them out. She smiled. It would be a while yet before the colt learned what hay was.

The bounty hunters led their animals to drink at the creek. Marshal Dexter stood with his animal outside the corral. She looked over at him, leaned the fork aside and went toward the colt. At first the mare was too hungry to look up but when Caitlin caught the colt around the neck and it squealed in fright the mare whirled with hay protruding from both sides of her mouth.

Caitlin was wrestling with the terrified colt. It made frightened noises. Dexter stood rooted. The men at the creek looked back.

The mare was fast when she whirled and lashed out. One hoof struck corral stringers. The men at the creek turned again, this time standing like statues.

Dexter moved with his horse to partially obstruct the view. The second time the mare lashed out Caitlin was bending over to maintain her grip and when the mare kicked she hit the colt and it screamed.

The mare's ears were pinned back. She was wildly angry. Caitlin saw her swing for her third kick and made no attempt to avoid the hoofs.

Because she was bending one hoof caught her low in the body, the other hoof came within inches of striking her head.

Dexter stopped breathing. Caitlin flung both arms up as she collapsed.

One of the men at the creek yelled for the marshal to shoot the mare. Dexter looped his reins and climbed between the stringers. The blow in the soft parts had been solid.

He waved his hat and the terrorized colt ran to its mother, the mare got between her baby and the kneeling lawman.

Caitlin was having trouble catching

her breath. She looked up and grimaced, then dropped flat on her face.

Art Waters was running toward the corral yelling like a bay steer. His partner also came back, leading two horses which hadn't fully tanked up and hung back.

Dexter tried to roll the tall woman over. She resisted. The pain was barely tolerable. She forced herself to speak. Dexter had to lean to hear. She said, 'The bottom of the wood box,' and turned limp.

The unpleasant bounty hunter was climbing into the corral when Dexter raised Caitlin's head and turned it, first to the left then to the right. As Waters came up, Dexter said, 'Broken neck,' and the unpleasant man retorted swiftly. 'Make her talk. Where's them bottles of gold.'

Dexter answered without looking up. 'Look in the cabin.'

Waters grunted back between corral stringers and called to the Texan. 'Her neck's broke,' and went in the direction of the cabin. The Texan had to tether the horses before he could follow.

When they were both in the house Dexter said, 'That was a fool thing to do.'

She didn't reply. The pain was still almost sickening in its intensity. He used his hat for a pillow. She pushed it away. 'Don't let them upend the wood box.'

He didn't move.

She swore at him, 'Damn it, keep them away from the wood box!'

He was getting to his feet when Art Waters emerged from the house with both arms around the bottles of gold. Will Roberts was behind him seemingly less interested in the tall woman's cache than in the round loaf of bread he was eating.

Art Waters ignored them all as he put the bottles in his oversized saddle-bags.

Dexter arose finally and went to the side of the corral, Waters finished buckling the saddle-bags and turned.

He was sweating and triumphant. 'Marshal, my partner will go down yonder with you for Coyle. They can catch up, I'll head north from here.' The bounty hunter smiled which did little to complement his normally hard expression. 'Will'll catch up . . . About Coyle . . . it's a long way. I've had 'em try to escape from me before. So has Will.' The unpleasant man's smile dwindled. For a moment he stood holding his reins then spoke again. 'Marshal, I got no use for your kind but I'll tell you straight out, it was good doin' business with you.'

Waters and the Texan conferred for a few minutes before Waters swung astride, reined easterly in the direction of the distant stage road and didn't look back.

The Texan came over and looked at the limp woman in the corral, ate some bread and said, 'Too bad. She'd've made someone a right handy cook an' for raisin' vegetables an' all. When you're ready we can head down yonder. I'd like to get Luther an' start back before it qets too dark.' He chewed while gazing in the direction of the forest. 'Are there bears an' cougars up here? If there is we could drag her carcass to the house.'

Dexter shook his head. 'It'll be all right, any varmint comes near the corral the mare'll run 'em off.'

Roberts continued to eat bread as he freed his animal and swung astride. When the marshal did not moved the Texan said, 'She was sweet on you,' and shook his reins for the animal under him to move out.

Dexter waited until the Texan had gone half across the clearing then said, 'Caitlin?'

'Yes.'

'I'll take you to the house.'

'No! Get astride and catch up with him. I'll be all right.'

'You're sure.'

'I'm sure. Come back tomorrow and bury me.'

157

If that was meant to be humorous Dexter didn't take it that way. He went after his horse, swung up and looked back. Caitlin raised a feeble wave. He waved back and followed the tracks left by the Texan.

He could hear the bounty hunter before he saw him. Roberts must have finished the bread, he was riding on a loose rein with his right hand braced against the swells. It was a downhill trail.

The Texan was one of those people whose sensibilities, like his conscience, had been ground out by a hard existence. When the marshal overtook him not far from open country he smiled and said, 'Art's a smart man. He'll have it all worked out when we get back up north.'

Dexter said nothing as he eyed the Texan. If Roberts ever saw his partner again it would be a miracle.

When they had rooftops in sight, the Texan squinted ahead when he said, 'That was dumb, her gettin' in the corral an' gettin' between the mare an' colt.'

Dexter saw lights up ahead when he nodded. 'Everybody makes mistakes.'

The Texan had said all he had to say on that subject. The closer they got to Winchester, the more he thought of Luther Coyle in the jailhouse. 'Marshal, you told us there'd have to be some kind of papers go around before you could hand Coyle over.'

Dexter's reply was almost careless. 'Special situations take special handlin'. You can have him. When you start back it'll be dark. I'd watch him real careful. He's a slippery son of a bitch.'

They left the animals with the liveryman's nighthawk to be hayed, grained, watered and cuffed. Roberts wanted to visit the eatery. Dexter went along, not enthusiastically even though he was also hungry.

When they entered the café there were three other diners. Even the caféman considered the marshal arriving with one of the strangers.

Dexter ordered for them both, nodded to the other diners and ignored the stare from the caféman when their coffee arrived.

As he was eating, it crossed his mind that as soon as the diners left they would head for the saloon. By the time Roberts was ready to ride north with Luther Coyle, word would have been passed.

When they left the eatery to cross to the jailhouse, the Texan said, 'Those gents wasn't real friendly actin' was they?'

Dexter was opening the jailhouse door when he answered. 'Most towns don't take to strangers right off.'

He had to stand on a chair to light the hanging lantern. As he was getting down the Texan asked if maybe he couldn't stay the night in one of the cells. He wasn't keen on riding north with Coyle in the dark.

Dexter dumped his hat atop the desk and shook his head. 'It'd be better to leave Winchester in an hour or so than to ride up the roadway with your prisoner in daylight when folks'll see you takin' him away.'

Evidently that logic had appeal. The Texan said, 'If you'll fetch the son of a bitch up here where I can go over him for hideouts, we can leave. By now Art's maybe ridin' down the far side of that big mountain.'

Dexter took his key ring, went down into the dark cell room, wordlessly unlocked the door and jerked his head. Luther, who previously'd had no trouble speaking, not only hesitated about leaving the cell but stared wordlessly at the marshal.

Dexter jerked his head again. 'Out. There's a gent up front who'll take you back up north.'

'Now, in the night?'

'Yes.'

'A lawman?'

'No, a bounty hunter. Come out of there!'

'Bounty hunter?'

'Out, Luther. *Come out!*'

Luther was reluctant, dragged his feet in the direction of the reinforced oaken cell-room door, opened it and looked around. The Texan returned his look as Dexter shoved Luther ahead. Where they stopped, Dexter introduced the men to each other. Luther took the Texan's measure through narrowed eyes.

Roberts spoke to the lawman. 'You go over him?'

'When he first came in. Do it yourself if it'd make you feel better.'

Roberts felt Luther then stepped back looking at the marshal. 'I can take him now?'

'Any time you want. There's somethin'; he don't have a horse. Maybe the liveryman'll sell you one.'

The Texan went to the door, opened it and jerked his head for Luther to precede him. When they were both outside, Dexter closed the door, sat at his desk until enough time had passed then he too went down to the livery barn where the proprietor was sucking his teeth after supper and told Dexter he'd sold one of those strangers a horse and outfit and watched them ride north up through town until it got too dark to see, then he had a word of advice when the marshal went after his animal.

'Leave him be, Mister Dexter. You been ridin' him pretty hard lately an' a horse ain't a machine. Take my buckskin, he's easy ridin' an' tougher'n an old boot.'

When Marshal Dexter left Winchester, also riding northward, he was astride a pig-eyed, un-pretty line-back buckskin horse with muscle where most horses didn't even have room for it.

9

Trapped!

By the time Dexter was riding up the trail to the tall woman's clearing, it was getting cold. He was passing through trees when he saw a soft light, the kind candles made. He left his horse with reins looped at the corral where the mare came over to nuzzle. She'd seen the marshal enough lately to accept him — outside the corral — inside she would have attacked him.

Dexter knocked on the door and instantly the candle was snuffed out. He knocked again and said his name.

When the tall woman opened the door, she was holding a shotgun in both hands. Dexter said, 'Good evenin', ma'am, I come up to do a buryin'.'

When he was inside where there was a warming fire she said, 'It's not morning yet,' and he nodded about that before replying.

'You didn't look good the last time I saw you.'

'You worried?'

'Yes'm. How do you feel?'

'Well, I'm better'n dead otherwise I feel like I been yanked through a knot hole.'

She made them coffee. She moved slowly and looked tired. He told her maybe he should get the medical man down in Winchester. Her reply was predictable. 'If I'm dead he can't do much, can he? Did you get rid of the Texan?'

'Got rid of both of 'em. The Texan an' Luther. If I was a guessin' man I'd say the Texan's no match for Luther but as far as we're concerned that's someone else's problem.'

She put her head slightly to one side as she told him he looked tired. He was tired, all the way to the marrow in his bones.

They sat at the table with their coffee

until she said, 'You're welcome to use the bed the storekeeper used,' and stood up. 'Good night, Marshal.'

He watched her cross to the bedroom and as her door was closed he eyed the cot, left his hat on the table, kicked out of his boots and tested the bed. It had springs and a lumpy mattress. The fire was burning low; the house was almost too warm as he removed his gun-belt and eased back.

It was the mare nickering that eventually awakened him. There was a fresh fire and a kettle of boiling water on the stove and shards of dawn light showing when he heaved up to the edge of the bed, pulled on his boots, vigorously scratched, got his hat, left the belt and holstered Colt where he'd hung them the night before, and was at the door to go outside when the gunshot scattered the silence.

He yanked open the door. The corralled mare was upset, his horse had been off-saddled, the rigging had been dumped outside the corral but the horse was nowhere in sight. Someone had set him afoot.

Caitlin Rourke called to him to get back inside and close the door which he did at about the time there was another shot. This time the bullet struck the door inches away, punched the door all the way open and strained its leather hinges. The second time he closed it he dropped the *tranca* into place and went after his shellbelt and holstered six-gun, went where Caitlin was half sitting, half lying on the cot. Until that moment he'd had no idea how ill she was, she had shown forced normalcy. One of the bullets had hit her in the side, had been deflected by a rib and had ploughed a course around her right side before exiting. She fainted.

He hesitated before removing her torn and bloody shirt. The wound consisted of ragged flesh which bled heavily.

He went to the stove for hot water, grabbed the first cloth he saw which was a dish towel, went back and wiped blood away to expose the damage.

What she needed was Doc Bedford. Dexter couldn't make the ride down and back and there was no way he could take her down yonder.

What he knew about injuries was limited to wire cuts on horses and personal injuries of minor concern.

He washed the wound again. Almost as fast as he did this fresh bleeding erupted. It was obvious that what had to be accomplished was to stop the bleeding.

He went to her bedroom, found a clean blouse, tore off the sleeves and made a compressed bandage. Blood showed through before he got the bandage tied.

She needed sewing; it required no vast experience with wounds to know that, but he'd never sutured even an animal.

Caitlin's period of unconsciousness was passing. She moaned. Dexter returned to the bedroom quickly, found a shirt, returned and covered

Caitlin's upper body.

She opened her eyes. He smiled as he said, 'You got shot. You need Doc Bedford from town but I dassn't leave you long enough to fetch him up here an' you can't make the trip down there.'

She spoke huskily. 'There's brandy in the cupboard-box on the wall next to the stove.'

He found the bottle and returned with it. She drank, made a grimace and as he retrieved the bottle she said, 'Who . . . ?'

He had no idea who had shot her or why. He ignored the question. 'You got neighbours?'

'No. Not that I know of an' I've hiked in all directions.'

'Are you hungry?'

She possibly understood his feeling of helplessness because she made a little smile. 'I'm not hungry, Marshal, but you are.'

Normally he would have been hungry but not now. 'Later,' he told her, and added more. 'I can't leave you'n I don't know what to do.'

She raised a hand to explore the bandage. It was tight, it was also soaked through, she let the hand fall. 'You did the best you knew to do.'

There was no denying that but it changed nothing, she was bleeding. If something wasn't done she would bleed to death.

He sat beside her on the bed feeling more useless than he'd ever felt in his life.

She read his expression and said, 'I'll make it. I've bled before. When I was building the cabin I . . . '

'What is it?'

'My mare. Listen.'

The noise was not loud. Clearly someone was in the corral. Dexter heard the squeal and the kick. He arose, crossed to the door and cracked it several inches. He recognized the man in the corral. Will Roberts, the Texan!

The mare was doing as she always

did when she thought there was a threat to her colt.

The Texan scrambled through the stringers. When he was safely outside breathing hard, a second man called from somewhere in the vicinity of the creek. 'Shoot the son of a bitch!'

The Texan turned facing the house. It was unlikely he could see the cracked-open door. The hidden man said it again, 'Shoot the damned mare!'

Instead the Texan faded from sight in the direction of the house. His limited vision made it impossible to see the other man.

Dexter eased the door closed, barred it as he spoke to the tall woman without looking in her direction. 'There's two of 'em. One's the Texan called Roberts. I can't see the other one but I'd guess it's Luther.'

He faced fully around. 'When I handed Luther over to Roberts down in town I didn't think the Texan was a match for anyone as slippery as Luther. Why are they up here?'

The tall woman was getting drowsy and didn't answer.

The marshal went to bedside; the bandage was thoroughly soaked. His feeling of helplessness returned as Caitlin spoke in a drowsy voice.

'There's baking powder in the cupboard. Get it.'

Dexter went to obey. When he returned Caitlin had to force herself to speak against the increasing drowsiness. 'Take the bandage off, wipe it clean. Before the bleedin' starts pour bakin' powder on the wound.'

He obeyed, emptied the can on to the wound then rebandaged it with the second blouse sleeve, and waited.

Blood showed through, but spottily, and with nowhere near the force it had bled through earlier.

Dexter put the can of baking powder aside and concentrated on watching.

Outside, someone was at the barred-door. He ignored the sound and leaned. The bleeding did not stop but it diminished and Caitlin slept. Her facial colour was grey, he felt for her heart. It was beating. He went after more hot water at the stove, filled a basin and washed.

It didn't require great intelligence to imagine why those men were out there. Will Roberts had seen his partner fill saddle-bags with jars of raw gold. From that conjecture it required only a second thought to suspect that the Texan had convinced the bounty hunter there would be more gold.

As soon as they crept close enough they had seen the marshal's tethered animal, one of them must have known he was riding the buckskin horse and set it afoot.

There was not a sound; someone had slipped up to the cabin perhaps with some idea of bursting inside which wouldn't have succeeded as long as the *tranca* was barring the door.

Dexter's primary concern was the tall woman. If a rib hadn't deflected the bullet she would have been killed. As he looked at her, he had a sinking sensation that she would die anyway.

The sun was climbing. Normally there would have been noisy birds. He heard none. Those gunshots would have sent them winging in all directions.

Caitlin softly said, 'The brandy, Mister Dexter.'

He got the bottle for her. When she handed it back he said, 'Folks call me Lex. That's my first name.' He might as well have spoken to a stone wall. She was asleep.

The spotty places had not spread and no fresh leaking showed. He was gratified without being too optimistic. She had lost considerable blood before it had slackened. She had no colour and when she spoke the words were slurred. He had no idea how much blood a person could lose before they died from the loss.

As he perched on the edge of the bed looking at her, he had a bad feeling.

A man with the unmistakable drawl of Texas called out. 'Marshal, you're afoot an' we can set you out if it takes a month. You hear me?'

Dexter did not reply.

'Marshal, you listen real good. Somethin' bad's goin' to happen to you. You got that dead woman in there? The same's goin' to happen to you. All's we got to do is fire the log house.'

Dexter saw Caitlin's colour improve. When her eyes were open they lacked the drowsy expression. She spoke in a stronger voice. Brandy was excellent medicine.

'What do they want?' she asked.

'My guess is they think you've got more jars of nuggets.'

'I don't have.'

'If you stood on a foot of Bibles I got an idea they wouldn't believe you.' Dexter smiled. 'The bleeding's about stopped.'

She ignored that. 'Let them in; they can search, there's no more gold.'

His reply was given in the tone someone might use to a child. 'If they ransacked an' found no gold they'd kill

175

us both for not findin' it.'

'And . . . ?'

He didn't have an answer. He leaned to examine the bandage which she watched him do and dryly said, 'They'll set fire, Marshal.'

He replied while very gingerly probing the bandage. 'They got to get close,' he said and stood up.

She watched him as he straightened up and said something that shocked him. 'You need a shave. I have a razor . . . Mister Dexter I'll owe you as long as I live. I don't think the law takes sides very often.'

Unaccustomed to that kind of talk made his face redden. He left her to go stand by the door straining to hear. There was not a sound and that worried him. The clearing was distant and isolated but that was no guarantee there couldn't be an interruption, townsmen had hunted Forest Mountain for years. Even as he had this hope he dismissed it. He and the tall woman were not going to be saved by an accident. Whatever happened in this hidden place would depend on the stalkers outside and the lawman inside.

He returned to bedside. Caitlin was asleep. He briefly listened to her even deep breathing then went exploring. The bedroom was large, the bedstead, a dresser of sorts with a cracked mirror and a handmade chair in front of a tall, wide closet were all handmade. He was impressed with the ingenuity and talent of their maker but what he sought, a window, did not exist except in the parlour between the door and the bed Caitlin occupied.

He examined three guns, a Winchester saddle gun, a double-barrelled shotgun and a horse pistol heavy enough to make an excellent hammer.

The window in the parlour had no glass, few outlying places had glass windows. It wasn't just the expense that precluded their use it was the wavery reflections. Caitlin's front wall window had a commonplace covering, rawhide scraped almost paper thin which permitted sunlight to show through but nothing else. She had made two wooden shutters with leather hinges to cover the window, something else which was common. It required several days of very careful scraping to thin-down rawhide.

He looked for chinking between the wall logs which had crumbled and had fallen out.

This was something else that impressed him. All his life he had seen log walls, always chinked and if they were old enough, minus strips of the mud used for chinking.

Not this time. There were places where the chinking had fallen, but every one of them had been rechinked.

He stood in the parlour. The only allies he had were the door and the window he could not see out of. While he was standing there a rock rattled against the front wall. It hadn't been hurled there with great momentum. One of the oldest known tricks was to make a noise whose purpose was to get a denned-up animal, or a two-legged one, to satisfy curiosity by poking a head out to look around.

Dexter went to the front wall and listened. There was silence. He was going to ease further along when a man called.

'Lawman, you got ten minutes. You come out an' you can ride away. You got my word we won't jump you. Ten minutes!'

Dexter was tempted to call back. Instead he yanked loose the tie down over his holster and went to look at Caitlin. She was awake. 'I'm sorry, Marshal. I'm sorry I got you into this.'

He smiled. 'Your colour's a little better.' He leaned to examine the bandage. Her body was swelling tightly against the bandaging but there was no fresh bleeding.

'Marshal?'

He looked at her, waiting.

'I don't think either of us is goin' to

walk away from this.' Before he could disagree she also said, 'Do you ever get lonely? I do. If things could have been different I'd have asked if you'd like livin' up here. There's good hunting. I know every creek'n lake. I've seen trout up here half as long as your arm. It's peaceful — well, most of the time.'

When she stopped speaking her eyes neither blinked nor wavered. Dexter felt heat in his face, waited until he could order the right words, and said, 'Caitlin . . . we'd ought to put off too much talkin', at least until we come out of this standin' up.'

She agreed instantly and turned her face to the wall. He briefly lingered, feeling uncomfortable, then went along the front wall again. The ten minutes were almost up. It did not surprise him when the man with the Texas accent called.

'Time's up, Marshal. You goin' to let us in or do we come in anyway, or set fire to the house an' shoot you when flames drive you out. *Time's up!*'

Dexter's answer was short. 'You can come in an' search. Leave the guns outside. I'll help you search.'

There was no response for several minutes then the caller had no accent when he said, 'You want to stay alive? All's you got to do is put the bottles of nuggets outside. That's all. We'll take 'em an' leave.'

Caitlin spoke from the bed. Her face was slightly flushed and sweat damp. 'The other one got all the bottles, but I have somethin' else: a buckskin pouch of fifty dollar gold pieces.'

Dexter stared at her.

'I took them from my husband's safe the night I left. There were four stacks of greenbacks. I didn't take them but right now I wish I had.'

Dexter sat down. If he offered them gold coins they would likely agree not to kill Caitlin and the marshal but sure as hell was hot they would kill them. He said, 'Caitlin, if you gave them the gold coins it'd make them all the more willin' to risk a fight to get inside and hunt for more gold, nuggets or coins. They'd kill us no matter what you gave them. They've got to kill us. As isolated as this place is we'd be skeletons before anyone found us an' they'd be long gone from here with new names.'

182

10

A Serious Wound

The sun was climbing, the sky was clear azure from horizon to horizon. There were no birds and wouldn't be until the clearing returned to normal.

There was a sound the marshal hadn't heard before. When he cocked his head, Caitlin sounded amused when she explained. 'There's a bee den in the back wall. That's what you hear. I never bother 'em an', they don't bother me.'

As time passed she seemed to rally, not much but noticeably. She asked a question. 'Is it a Mexican stand off?'

He nodded; it was as long as they were forted up inside, at least until their attackers started a fire outside.

He asked how old the log house was. She said she'd completed it two years earlier and followed that up by saying, 'Why?'

He answered almost cryptically. 'Dry logs burn, green ones don't.'

Nothing more was said until she surprised him by being hungry. He knew how to make broth from jerky and made her a pan full. It wasn't the best substitute for a meal but it would do, for awhile anyway.

He took his cup to bedside, she sipped and thought out loud. 'They'd be crazy to try it.'

'Try what?'

'Burn us out in broad daylight.'

She sent him after another cup of broth and complimented him on making it. He returned with the cup and one for himself. As she took the cup he seated himself on the edge of the bed as she also said, 'I expect if I had to choose someone to be forted up with it'd be you.'

He turned his cup using both hands, without speaking or looking at her. Eventually he gazed at the riddled door and said, 'Likely they'll wait until dark,' dropped his gaze to her bandaging and made an offhand remark. 'I never heard of usin' bakin' powder to stop bleeding,' and her reply startled him.

'Neither did I but I've used clear dirt an' spider webs. We don't have anything like that, do we?'

He restlessly paced to the door, cracked it a few scant inches, closed it, put the bar in place and paced as far as the cooking area and her bedroom. When he returned Caitlin was asleep. He retrieved her empty cup, put them both on the pine wood counter near the stove and resumed his pacing.

They were still out there. They wouldn't leave until they got inside to ransack, which in all probability would help them find her cache of gold coins.

He tried a ruse. Opening the door a fraction he called out. 'There's riders comin'.' He got no answer but a loud laugh. He tried again, 'When I don't show up in town they'll be lookin' for me.'

This time he got a reply. 'You think we're greenhorns? Nobody's comin' an' if they did we could see 'em. Marshal, you don't have a choice. Toss out your gun an' come where we can see you. I told you before, you got my word there'll be no shootin'.'

Dexter answered shortly. 'Mister, I wouldn't take your word if you was standin' on your mother's grave.'

The speaker laughed again. 'I said you got no choice. Come dark we'll make you run out of there.'

Caitlin spoke from the cot. 'Marshal, help me up.'

He turned as she tried to sit up. He crossed toward her in long strides, leaned and pushed her down and held her down. 'You'll start the bleeding,' he growled, and her answer was candid.

'It'd be better than dying in bed.'

The Texan called. 'Marshal?'

When Dexter didn't reply the Texan said, 'Find where she hid gold and toss it outside an' we'll be gone. Don't do it an' we'll roast you alive.'

Caitlin said, 'Under the bed are four short boards. The money is under them.'

Dexter didn't make the search, he went back to the rawhide window, worked a corner loose and peeked out. The afternoon was waning. He saw no one as he raised the bullhide until it was high enough, pushed his fisted six-gun through and let go a wild shot in the direction of the creek.

The response came from the direction in which he had fired and also from around a corner of the mare's shed. Both bullets struck the rawhide. Dexter had barely a moment to drop the rawhide and jump sideways to flatten against the wall.

Caitlin looked steadily at him without making a sound. He had determined where the attackers were at the moment they returned his fire which simply meant they would not be in the same places if he fired again.

Luther made his derisive laugh. 'Go ahead, Marshal, you got four bullets left.'

Caitlin said, 'The carbine is loaded. Fire your pistol empty and get the carbine.'

Dexter waited several minutes then poked his six-gun past the rawhide and fired four shots. This time the returned gunfire not only came from a different place it also showed that Luther and Will Roberts were together.

Dexter got Caitlin's saddle gun, moved the slide to be sure the weapon was charged and had finished doing that when Luther called.

'You got her guns in there. I saw 'em a couple days ago. Try again, Marshal.' Luther followed this up with a random shot that tore the rawhide window covering.

Will Roberts was on the north side of the cabin with a clear view southward. He was reloading when something made him look up and he turned to stone.

There were riders filtering among the trees southward. He called to Luther and raised a rigid arm. Luther swore.

Their animals were tethered behind the mare's shed. To reach them they would have to run from the north side of the house across cleared ground to the corral. Luther jerked his head for the Texan to follow and went along the side of the house to the strip of grassland clearing, more open ground but the house would be between the two men until they could reach the forest. If the horsemen came into the clearing in the direction of the house they would be unable to see the fleeing men. It wasn't a matter of choice it was a matter of urgency.

Those horsemen among the trees were wary, but the pair of renegades were about half the distance to the trees when the westernmost horseman saw them running, let out a yell and hooked his horse in pursuit.

Luther heard pursuit, twisted and fired from the hip. His companion passed Luther. He neither paused nor looked back.

The horseman who had been Luther's target fired as Luther lengthened his stride as he ran. Neither shooter hit his target, but shortly before they reached the trees, sucking air as anyone would do who wasn't accustomed to running on foot, three other riders came after them.

The Texan reached timber and paused to look back. A bullet struck a huge fir tree about a foot to one side and the Texan sprang into the air and lit down running.

One of the horsemen yelled, 'Get around 'em!' and two riders veered southward and hooked their mounts.

The marshal and Caitlin Rourke heard the gunfire, the pounding sound of running horses and wondered until Dexter cracked the door, saw one horseman pass from sight around the north side of the house and recognized him.

He turned and said, 'Nat Bedford.'

At the blank look he got from the tall woman he added more. 'The doctor from Winchester.'

A very brief but furious series of gunshots erupted north-west of the house as Luther set a roundabout course in the direction of the shed where their horses were tethered.

He didn't make it. A burly, balding man cut Luther off and ran at him. Both men fired. The Texan also fired, but he had been lagging, his legs ached and his lungs burned. He hadn't moved fast on foot in years. His shot at the horsemen was close, it clipped a small low tree limb.

Luther's shot was closer, it made the burly man lean in the saddle.

The burly man's shot ploughed dirt and needles a few feet in front of Luther. The effect was to make Luther jam to an abrupt halt.

He was recovering from being peppered with dirt, small stones and needles when the burly man reined slightly to one side and threw himself from the saddle. He and Luther went down, dust flew, Luther squawked and the Texan was shifting in order to get a clear shot at the burly man when two riders appeared, one on each side. They reined to a halt with handguns aimed and cocked.

The Texan who lacked a lot of being the most perceptive soul on earth didn't have to be, he dropped his six-gun.

Luther fought like a cougar, he was fast and agile. He lacked something like thirty pounds of matching his adversary in weight as well as the burly man's strength. Blacksmiths grew muscles without effort.

The bald man rolled until Luther was beneath him before wrenching Luther half upwards and hit him hard.

Luther sagged like a sack of wet grain.

The riders herded the Texan in the direction of the cabin. The blacksmith half dragged, half carried Luther whose mouth was bleeding.

The horsemen dismounted in front of

the house and one called out, 'It's Arnie Buscomb, Fred Muller, Doc Bedford an' Josh Hanson, the preacher.'

Dexter opened the door. The townsmen herded Luther and his companion inside. Doc Bedford went to Caitlin. So did the storekeeper who was appalled. Doc may have also been appalled but he didn't show it as he went to work.

Doc jerked his head for help and they carried Caitlin to her bedroom, doc shooed the others out and went to work.

The blacksmith sidled up to Marshal Dexter. 'Good thing for you that buckskin horse come runnin' down the middle of the road. He went to the livery barn. The liveryman would have come except he had to do chores. Marshal, you never should've turned that horsethief over to that bounty hunter.'

Dexter agreed without saying so. He considered the prisoners on the bench with the table at their backs. Luther's face was swelling and changing colour. Neither of them looked at the men who seemed to fill the cabin. When Caitlin had made her home it hadn't been with any idea of having a crowd of visitors.

The preacher calmly and methodically went over the prisoners, one had a boot knife, the other had a hide-out derringer.

Doctor Bedford emerged from the bedroom, stood with his back to the door unrolling his sleeves when he said, 'The wound'll heal given time. It's the blood she lost that worries me.' He shifted his gaze to the captives. 'Which one of you sons of bitches shot her?'

Both Luther and the Texan stoutly denied being guilty and Dexter told the townsmen and the doctor the bullet had ricocheted from outside when both men had been firing.

The burly blacksmith had the solution for handling men who would shoot a woman. 'Hang 'em both.'

The preacher and the storekeeper

went to care for their animals. Their absence lessened the sensation of crowding in the parlour. It also offered an opportunity for the marshal to question the captives. He started out by saying there were no more nuggets in the house. He then told them when they got down to Winchester he would lock them up and write up charges until the circuit riding judge came to town, which might be a month, maybe longer. He had a purpose. He told the Texan that by the time he got free, if he did, his partner in bounty hunting would be safe up north with all the bottles of gold, and if he was a guessing man he'd guess the Texan would never see his partner again nor his share of the gold.

The Texan listened without interrupting, his gaze fixed on the marshal and when Dexter walked away the Texan's gaze followed him.

He would get his share of the gold if he had to hunt his partner to hell and back and he would shoot him if his share wasn't all there.

The blacksmith said he had to get back. The others agreed; they all had reasons for getting back. They would take the prisoners back with them and lock them up in the jailhouse. Only Doc Bedford wouldn't ride with the others. It would be several days before he thought he could safely leave the tall woman.

Dexter went to the bedroom, Caitlin smiled and held out a hand. He used the bedside chair Doc Bedford had used, squeezed her fingers and asked what Doc Bedford had said. She answered candidly.

'A person can only lose so much blood. He won't know if I've passed that point for several days.'

'Did he say how he would know?'

She nodded. 'A person gets weaker, listless, can't move much and don't want to. Marshal? If you could stay a spell, I won't be able to get out to feed my mare.'

He squeezed her fingers. 'For as long

as you want me to stay,' and left the room when she dozed off.

Doctor Bedford had made coffee, filled two cups and took them to the table, sat down and looked straight at the marshal. 'She's healthy, strong as a bull but . . . ' The coffee was too hot, he pushed the cup away. 'Lex, she bled a lot. I don't know. We'll just have to wait. When I go back is there anyone who can look after her?'

Dexter nodded. 'I will.'

Doctor Bedford may have anticipated this answer because he said, 'An' who'll mind things in town?'

Dexter's reply was blunt. 'There's plenty who can do that.'

'I'll tell the council. They'll likely want to know how long you'll be up here.'

'As long as I have to be, Nat.'

The physician tried the coffee, it wasn't too hot. He drank it and arose. 'There's a mare in the corral needs feeding.'

Dexter went to the corral with the

doctor. They fed the mare, Doc Bedford admired the colt and as they were outside leaning on stringers he said, 'Lex, I'm not real hopeful.'

Dexter said nothing.

The doctor was curious. 'Why did those bastards come up here?'

'She gave some jars of nuggets to the other one, the manhunter named Art Waters. He left with them in his saddle-bags. The one with the Texas accent was to go to town, get Luther and catch up. My guess is that Luther told the bounty hunter there was more gold up here, most likely in the house. Him an' the bounty hunter came along to get it.'

'Damned good thing your horse came back to town all lathered from runnin' home.'

Dexter had nothing to say about that. His thoughts were elsewhere.

'Does she have a chance; tell me straight out.'

The physician leaned on the corral stringer eyeing the mare and colt. 'If she does, it'll be a slim one. She lost a lot of blood.' He turned, 'Make her eat; get meat broth down her. The rest is — wait. That's all I can tell you. I'll come back when I can. Lex? She's fond of you.'

Dexter also considered the mare and colt when he replied, 'I'm fond of her.'

The physician gave Dexter a light slap on the arm turned in the direction of the house. 'I'll tell her to mind what you say then be on my way.'

Dexter lingered at the corral. Later, when the physician came to get his horse they exchanged a nod without a word and Doctor Bedford crossed out of the clearing into the timber. The sun was sinking. By the time he got back to Winchester it would be dark.

Dexter pitched another flake of hay to the mare and went to the house. He knew little about cooking but he was going to learn.

Caitlin slept a lot. She dutifully drank the broth he made and picked at the food. He made her smile when he explained his difficulties with preparing meals. She told him he was doing right well and was asleep before he closed the door after himself.

He slept on the cot in the parlour, hauled water from the creek, spent time with the mare until she accepted his presence in the corral but when he tried to teach the colt to lead, the mare didn't like that. Twice she chased him out of the corral with bared teeth and ears laid back.

He explored but never for long. He fed Caitlin broth until she eventually balked and told him how to boil potatoes, melt goat cheese to slather them in, and after a week they ate together in her bedroom. What he didn't know was that she was not a hearty eater. He did his best to make meals he thought she would like. She did her best to eat them but her appetite was slow to improve. He blamed that on his inability to cook, so did she, but wild horses couldn't have made her tell him that.

When she had a good day she would call out instructions to him at the stove. On the sixth day she laughed when he brought her meal. He had arranged springs of wild mint around the platter's edge but she still only picked at the food. She had no difficulty with broth, mainly because she liked broth.

Doctor Bedford came up leading Dexter's horse which he hobbled in the meadow before coming to the house.

He offered no greeting, just raised his eyebrows. Caitlin heard them talking and called. Doc Bedford looked startled. He went to the bedroom leaving Dexter at the parlour table. If the physician hadn't closed the door Dexter would have been able to eavesdrop, as it was he got himself another cup of coffee and stoically waited.

When Bedford returned he closed the bedroom door after himself, rolled down his sleeves, brought his satchel to the table with him and said, 'Whose idea was that, using baking powder to stop the bleeding?'

The marshal set a cup of coffee in front of the physician before answering. 'There wasn't anythin' else.'

Bedford tasted the coffee, put the cup aside and dryly said, 'If you can't cook any better'n you make coffee I'd better find a woman to come up here.'

Dexter ignored that. 'Is she any better?'

'She's better.' Doc leaned on the table. 'Do you have any idea how long her recovery will take? She won't be able to walk outside by herself until about Christmas time.'

'But she's on the mend?'

'Yes Lex, I wouldn't have bet a lead cartwheel she'd make it.'

'You sound more hopeful than that last time you come up here.'

Doctor Bedford showed a rueful little smile. 'In my business a man learns real early to be right careful with the truth. When in doubt lie a little. I brought a roll of bandaging an' some ointment. Don't let her catch cold. You're doing a good job.' The medical man arose. 'Thanks for the coffee; I've got to get back.' Bedford paused gazing steadily at the marshal. 'The council voted to replace you. I talked myself blue in the face. I might as well have peed in a creek expecting it to raise the water level.'

They went to Doc's animal, he tested the cinch, found it satisfactorily snug and mounted. As he was reining around southerly, he said, 'Arnie came up with an idea. Make a grave in the cemetery with her name on the headboard. Just in case some other bounty hunters come along . . . Lex, you're doing a good job. I'll come back when I can an' bring more bandaging. Don't let her leave that bed.'

Dexter lingered in the dying day until he could no longer see the physician or his horse then returned to the house. Caitlin heard him close the door and called.

He was startled when he entered the bedroom, her hair was pulled back and fixed into an upward braid, her face was shiny and the colour was good. She wanted to know what the doctor had said. He sat on the chair while he told her. When he mentioned the idea of sending a woman up from Winchester to maybe decently cook and help, Caitlin's response was swift and strong.

'No! I don't need someone else.'

'But a woman could cook better for you.'

'You're a good cook. Please, don't let anyone come up here. We're doin' fine. What did he say about my recovery?'

'Maybe by Christmas time you can walk as far as the corral.'

She considered him pensively. 'You'll leave before then.'

'Most likely not. The town council's lookin' for someone to take my place.'

'Lex, it's my fault. I should have gone down there to be looked after.'

He arose grinning. 'To be right

honest with you, I was tired of breakin'
up dog fights, throwin' drunks in jail
overnight, climbing trees to get some
widow-woman's cat down . . . You
ready for some broth?'

She inclined her head slowly and
watched him leave the room. He hadn't
said anything about her hair. She'd
dragooned the doctor to help put it
up.

11

Candour

Lex Dexter lost track of time which for him was nothing unusual. Doctor Bedford came up twice more to leave bandaging and ointment. He told Caitlin she wound have one hell of a scar, that the wound should have been sewn but there was no surgeon he knew of within a two week ride.

Her retort was what he might have expected if he had known her better. 'I have other scars, they don't bother me. Is it healing well?'

'Better and quicker than I expected. Caitlin, your hair's kind of scraggly.'

She smiled and nodded as he arose to make the braid under her instructions. When he finished he said, 'In a month maybe you'll be able to do it yourself, just don't keep your arms

206

raised very long and whatever you do, don't strain.'

Being a forthright individual she asked how much she owed him and he shrugged. 'Someday. When you come ridin' to town we'll do some figuring. I won't be back unless you send for me, but I'll be watchin' the road.'

In the parlour with the bedroom door closed, Doctor Bedford said, 'Lex, the council hired Fred Muller as new town marshal,' and held out his hand. Dexter put the badge on the outstretched palm. Doc pocketed the badge and stood impassively regarding Dexter. 'I've heard of it happening before. A patient getting mighty fond of a nurse, but I never knew a male nurse before.'

They went to Doc's horse and as Doc mounted, he said, 'You could do a lot worse,' and rode across the clearing to disappear into the forest.

He would be back sooner than he was expected but as Dexter watched him out of sight he couldn't anticipate that.

Time passed. Eventually Caitlin could leave the bed. She was as weak as a kitten. Her legs seemed to have forgotten what feet were for but after a couple more weeks she didn't need his help.

He went hunting with her saddle gun two days in a row before he saw a large tom turkey in a tree, shot it and brought it back.

They sat outside plucking it. He said he thought she needed a dog and she agreed as she arose to take the plucked bird inside to be cooked.

They feasted. She asked if he would help her put up her hair. He agreed with misgivings. He lacked the kind of ability except for the braiding. He'd been plaiting since childhood. The rest of it not only made him uncomfortable but her best instructions were translated by a former lawman who was all thumbs.

Autumn brought chilly nights, falling leaves except among the pines and firs, and long Vs of geese heading south sent faintly heard raucous calls earthward.

The colt occasionally sucked; the mare was drying up; their association was still mother and child but different than it had been.

When Dexter taught the colt to lead, the mare watched but that was all she did.

Caitlin went as far as the shed and appeared with a curved handled scythe. When Dexter asked what she was going to do she replied shortly, 'Cut grass in the meadow to winter the mare and colt.' She smiled at him. 'Come along, I'll show you how it's done.'

Out where grass heads were making seeds she swung the scythe and he stopped her, took the scythe and said he'd do it.

She didn't argue but hid a smile with her hand as she watched and finally said, 'Did you ever cut hay before?'

He hadn't.

'Let me show you. When you swing it you turn with the swing an' you tip the blade just a tad. Like this.'

He stopped her again and took back the scythe. She went into the shade and watched. When she was satisfied he had grasped the way scythes were used she sat on a stump, told him he was doing right well, and settled on the grass below the stump to nap.

That night he bathed at the creek and grimaced. He ached in places he didn't know he had. There was a science to using a scythe; it required the kind of physical effort he was unfamiliar with.

She teased him at supper. They laughed and when they parted, Caitlin in the direction of her bedroom, Dexter in the direction of the cot, she hesitated in her doorway looking back. He told her good night and kicked out of his boots. She closed the door.

Two days later Arnie Buscomb rode up. He was not carrying a creel nor the tube for his fishing pole. They visited for a while before the storekeeper said, 'I got this idea of making a grave in the cemetery outside of town, put a headboard up saying 'Here Lies Caitlin Rourke'.' Buscomb paused. 'Someday someone might come along like those bounty hunters did. Folks in town could show 'em the grave.'

Dexter had heard this idea mentioned before. As Caitlin brought cups of coffee he said, 'Arnie, Caitlin would still be around. If a stranger was interested he could find out she wasn't in the grave.'

Buscomb looked at Caitlin for support. She said, 'It's a good idea but folks know who I am an' where I live.'

The storekeeper slumped. 'That's what Rebecca said, among other things. Her opinion was that I'd better just keep to runnin' the store.'

Caitlin took him to the corral, showed how well the colt was coming along and said, 'I'm obliged, Mister Buscomb.'

He was defensive. 'I thought maybe it'd help to keep nosy folks from botherin' you.'

They fed Buscomb and his horse. He

didn't leave until the sun was lowering and after he was gone Caitlin said, 'That's part of why I don't want to have to leave. I've never had many friends. Real friends.'

They went outside in the gloaming, leaned on the corral stringers and were ignored by the mare and nuzzled by the colt.

They had been together several months. Dexter mentioned this before also saying, 'I like it when you laugh,' and faced her as solemn as an owl. She was not an inhibited person, by nature she was direct and forthright. She said, 'I said I'd like for you to stay.'

He returned his attention to the nuzzling colt. His response was candid. 'In about three years your colt's got to be altered.'

She faintly frowned, led the way to the house with dusk settling. As he lighted candles and the overhead lamp, she watched him in something like exasperated silence.

Two days later he took the carbine

to go hunting. She said she would accompany him. He was doubtful. 'It's a lot of walking.'

'We could take your horse and ride double.'

His horse had never been ridden double. Some horses objected to a pair of two-legged things on their backs. He mentioned this and the possibility of her injury being troublesome if she got bucked off.

She didn't argue, she said, 'I'll walk beside the horse.'

He showed displeasure at this. Squaws walked beside mounted buck Indians. He'd seen this many times and hadn't like it.

He compromised. 'We'll walk.'

It was cool despite a high-standing sun. Among the forest giants it was downright cold. She wore a blanket coat, he had his leather jacket with sheep-pelt lining. She had no gloves so he gave her his.

A light wind blew until they reached the windbreaking timber.

They rested often, covered a fair distance without finding edible game. They encountered a 600 pound black bear who was so occupied tearing bark in his search for grubs he was unaware of their presence until they were close. It was a surprise for the bear as well as for the two-legged creatures.

There was a Mexican standoff for a full minute before the bear decided to leave which it did without haste, grumbling and whining as it went, occasionally looking back.

Caitlin said, 'Two hundred pounds of meat,' and Dexter looked at her sharply.

'They're carrion eaters.'

'You've never eaten bear meat?'

'No, and I've seen dozens of them, mostly when they've found an old carcass.'

They completed a big circle without seeing anything to shoot and were coming from the north toward the clearing when they heard the mare squeal.

They advanced cautiously, saw the riderless tethered horse at the corral and stopped in tree gloom. Caitlin did not recognize the animal but Dexter did. It was the animal of Fred Muller, the blacksmith. Muller had replaced Dexter as town marshal.

Dexter had a bad feeling; he and the blacksmith were friends but sometimes authority changed people. He told Caitlin to wait and walked into sight west of the corral and horse shed.

The balding, burly man was at the cabin door. Dexter called and Muller turned and called back. 'With no one around I was scairt I'd made the ride for nothing.'

Caitlin appeared from the forest. Muller nodded but faced Dexter as he said, 'I sure could use some coffee.'

His attitude was not hostile. It wasn't even as uncomfortable as it would be between a man of authority and someone he might be seeking in his official capacity.

When they were inside with Caitlin

making coffee, the blacksmith sat at the table as he said, 'Ma'am, you look real good. Last time I saw you I wouldn't have bet a cartwheel you'd make it.'

Caitlin brought the coffee, sat opposite the blacksmith next to Dexter and was quiet. Muller sipped coffee before speaking.

'There's a problem. Ma'am, do you know a man named Carl Ames?'

Caitlin woodenly nodded.

'He's in Winchester with a couple of rangemen askin' questions about you.'

Caitlin lost colour and seemingly the ability to speak. The new town marshal told them the rest of it. 'Seems them bounty huntin' strangers was friends of his. They never come back. He traced 'em to Winchester.'

Dexter had a stray thought. The unpleasant manhunter, Art Waters, had had plenty of time to get back up north and report to the man who had hired him to find Caitlin. Evidently he hadn't returned to report to his employer.

Those bottles of nuggets and the

long ride back had sure as hell's hot convinced him not to go back, to go somewhere else and lose himself. That shouldn't have surprised Dexter and it didn't.

Muller spoke again, 'I told him we'd had the one that talked like Texas in our jailhouse. I told him we had both his bounty hunter and a stage robber locked up. He wanted to talk to the Texan. I told him he come too late.

'He didn't like that very well. I'd guess where he come from he cuts a lot of mustard.' The blacksmith arose, emptied his cup, dug out a large pocket watch, flipped it open, consulted the little spidery hands, pocketed the watch and said, 'I got to get back. Ma'am, thank you for the hospitality.'

Dexter went to the corral where Muller's animal was tethered. As the town marshal was unlooping his reins Dexter spoke.

'Ames is the father of Caitlin's husband that she shot when he was beatin' up on her.'

217

Muller nodded from the saddle as though he'd already heard that story and said, 'He'll find out where this place is. If I was in your boots I'd take the lady and get as deep into the mountains as I could get an' wait him out.'

Dexter returned to the cabin after the blacksmith was no longer in sight and found Caitlin at the table with her head in her arms. She wasn't making a sound but her slumped look of despair spoke volumes.

He tossed his hat aside, sat opposite her at the table and quietly said, 'Ames's got to be a vindictive feller. It's a long ride to here. Longer if you figure how much stoppin' an' askin' around he'd have to do.'

Caitlin neither raised her head nor spoke.

Dexter's feeling of helplessness drove him outside to the corral where he forked feed and leaned in shade watching the animals. He didn't hear her approach until she spoke.

'They told me he'd never give up.'

She leaned beside him looking at the horses. He didn't like her mood or her expression so he spoke frankly. 'The blacksmith's right; he'll find this place.'

She said nothing except to murmur in the direction of the colt. When she eventually turned he saw the tears. For seconds, he experienced a sensation he couldn't recall ever feeling before.

He reached to put a hand on her shoulder and she flung herself into his arms and this time made no attempt to hide the sobs.

He took her to the cabin, to the place where they sat along the front wall, eased her down, fished for his bandanna and pushed it into her hand.

She was a tough woman. It wasn't just the arrival of her dead husband's father that upset her, it was also something she would live with all her life, the expression on her husband's face when she shot him. The toughest women were more sensitive than men realized.

She used the bandanna, then smiled at him. He made a statement to her straight from the heart.

'If he comes up here he just might spend eternity here.'

She was drying her face when she shook her head. 'No. Lex, he was dead set against his son marryin' me. I had nothing. He wanted something better for Jess. But we got along. One time when Jess's father couldn't catch his horse in our corral he got so mad his face was red. I roped the horse and handed him the lariat. He saddled up and left for town without so much as a thank you. Three days later he sent a man from town with a little package for me. It was the most beautiful solid silver bracelet you ever saw. Jess threw it in the well. That was the morning he started drinkin'. In the afternoon he knocked me down, lifted me up an' flung me across the room.

'He went after the bottle in the cupboard. I knew he'd come back, got his pistol and when he came, screaming at me and hit me again, I shot him.'

Dexter waited until her eyes were dry before saying, 'It's gettin' cold.'

They went inside, he built a fire and she went to the stove. He told her he wasn't hungry.

They sat a long time in silence with dusk passing and darkness settling. Coyotes sounded; he thought they were too close and went outside with the six-gun shoved into the front of his britches.

The coyotes were somewhere between the corral and the darkened forest northward.

He waited a long time but they must have caught man-scent because the next time they sounded it was deep within the forest.

He remained outside for awhile. There were legions of stars in a perfectly clear sky which meant it would freeze before morning.

When he got back inside, Caitlin was sitting on the cot staring into the fire. He shoved the six-gun back into its holster and sat beside her. She sounded as though she were talking to herself when she said, 'Everything here I did myself an' broke two axe handles, got some lumps. It's my home. The animals are my family.' She looked around. 'Do you believe there's a law of retribution?'

He shrugged without replying; he'd never thought about it.

'There must be,' she softly said. 'But Jess would have killed me.'

Lex poured them both a bit of brandy and sat down beside her, raised his glass and swallowed just once. He knew what the result would be, and it was. His eyes watered, his throat burned and his breathing was limited to short inhalations and equally as short exhalations.

She downed the brandy, put the glass aside and gasped. 'I brought it with me. I should've brought whiskey.'

He could have agreed but instead he said, 'You know Forest Mountain pretty well?'

She didn't reply immediately and when she did she also shook her head. 'If you mean, hide. I've got to face it, Lex; hidin' means it'll never be settled.'

'I'll ride down yonder an' look him up.'

'He won't be alone.'

'I know; he's got a pair of rangemen with him.'

'Lex . . . stay here . . . please?'

The brandy was working. If there'd been whiskey he'd have got himself another couple of swallows. 'I'll get between you an' him. Caitlin, I got no idea how this happened, but bein' up here lookin' after you'n all. Walkin' with you, when we laughed . . . '

'Yes?'

'I know you hate men.'

'I hated one man.'

'Well . . . it's about time we bedded down, isn't it?'

She looked at him a long moment before placing one of her hands atop one of his hands, arose and said, 'Good night.'

He waited an hour, listened to the coyotes in the far distance, went to the door, startled a small owl which made an abrupt hooting sound and fled on silent wings.

His horse was dozing in moonlight, full as a tick. It didn't move while he removed the hobbles and used them to lead the animal in the direction of the place where his outfit was.

He bridled first, flung the blanket over next and boosted the saddle into place. It was late and it was cold. Because the bit in the horse's mouth was cold it rolled the cricket with its tongue. That was the only sound. Horsemen never mounted a cold-backed horse so he led the animal in the direction of the cabin before mounting.

He turned it once, raised his left foot to the stirrup and a pale ghost in the cabin doorway said, 'Lex, no. Please.'

He hadn't seen her nor heard a sound until she spoke. He hung, briefly prepared to swing astride when she spoke again. 'If I lose you I'll lose everything . . . please don't.'

He got both feet on the ground gazing at her across the saddle seat. 'Caitlin, if I get down there an' surprised him . . . '

'Three against one?' she said quietly. 'Wait here with me. If something happens to you I'll be alone when they come.'

He leaned on the horse. She appeared as something almost eerie in her white nightdress as motionless as a statue.

He knelt, hobbled the horse, arose to remove the saddle and blanket and finally the bridle. The horse hobble-hopped in the direction of the meadow. He was experienced at moving like that. An experienced horse wearing no hobbles could hop faster than most men could run.

She stepped aside for him to enter. The house was warm, the fire was down to embers. She lighted two candles, disappeared in her bedroom and reappeared wearing a robe. In the weak light they both looked younger.

She said, 'Coffee?' and he shook his head while watching her.

She came to the table, sat across from him and spoke quietly without moving her eyes from his face. 'We've lived here since early summer.' She reddened a little but he couldn't make that out as she continued speaking without lowering her eyes from his face. 'Lex?'

'Yes.'

'Will you marry me? I know you're used to town living, but you'd get to love this place the way I do . . . Lex?'

He was surprised but there was also an indefinable emotion. Years later he might try to recall and define it but right then he didn't make the effort.

She mistook his silence to be hesitation, maybe even rejection of the idea, and said, 'I can show you where to pan for nuggets. We'd put up enough hay from the meadow for your horse.'

He let out a long silent sigh and smiled. 'For some weeks I've wondered if you'd run me off if I said that.'

Their hands met atop the table, the fire burned, the candles made shadows on the walls and those coursing coyotes sounded again, this time at the moon. They were so distant their singing was faint.

'Lex?'

'Caitlin, the man's supposed to ask, not the woman.'

She smiled. By candlelight it was the smile of a young girl. 'Ask,' she said, and they both laughed. He wouldn't know for years that she was as nervous as he was.

'You've come to be part of me, Caitlin. I wanted very much to take care of you. I, uh, I've been in love for you since last summer.'

'Why didn't you say something?'

'Well, you did all this without a man. I figured you wouldn't like me saying . . . '

She squeezed his fingers so hard he flinched. She removed her hand immediately and he said, 'See, that's what I mean. You're . . . '

'Self-sufficient, Lex? Lonely and sad an' sort of scairt. Not of you, but of everyone else. I went down yonder for supplies, but they were all strangers. I'd come back and talk to the mare. I helped her have the colt. I got no idea who the stud was.'

He smiled. 'I expect she don't know either.'

'I didn't know she was heavy when I bought her. She an' I raised the colt. We mothered him . . . Sometimes I'd cry I was so lonely and afraid. An' now I expect I'm goin' to have to pay for it. It's not your trouble. It might be better if I'd let you ride down there, except if they killed you I couldn't stand that. I don't want any more nightmares an' sorrows.'

He arose, leaned far over and kissed her, sat back down and the poor light hid his high colour.

She started to cry. Dutifully he pushed the bandanna over as he said, 'Don't do that.'

She smiled through her tears, lustily blew her nose and nodded in the direction of the bullet-riddled rawhide window covering.

It was dawn. He would have known that without looking at the window. The mare nickered. She was always fed about daybreak.

He arose to go pitch feed. She brushed his arm as he passed.

Outside it was cold, he had to use a boot heel to break the skiff of ice where the mare drank.

Cold or not he lingered to consider the fading stars, the giant, dark, humpbacked distant rim of Forest Mountain and blew out a noisy long breath.

The damnedest things happened to a man when he wasn't expecting them.

Caitlin was dressed and working at the stove when he returned. She said, 'You forgot your coat.'

He had for a fact. He watched her at the stove wondering if that's what wives did, remind their men what they should have done.

They ate heartily. Dexter surprised himself, while he'd been outside food had been the furthest thing from his mind.

She had finished eating and was coddling her coffee cup when she said, 'You didn't answer.'

He chewed, swallowed and looked across the table. She was regarding him with an almost solemnly grave expression. He said, 'I didn't know I had to answer, but, ma'am, yes I'd marry you if that wound had put you in bed for life.'

She arose, swiftly removed their plates and kept her back to him in the area of the stove. When eventually she turned her eyes were bright and wet. She said, 'Take a walk with me.'

They went across the clearing where his horse watched them pass with minimal interest, entered the forest and while holding his hand she guided him on a course she was familiar with. It ended beside a cold-water creek. She released his hand and knelt. He knelt beside her and watched as she plunged an arm into the water, stirred silt, arose as she withdrew her hand, trickled water through the fingers, leaned down and using one finger poked in the mud.

He saw the tiny flakes. She washed them away in the water and looked around.

'A mile or so farther up the flakes are atop the mud, the nuggets are deeper in the mud.'

They sat in creek-side grass protected from the low, light cold breeze that was stirring mane and tail hair among the horses.

She said, 'That's my dowry.'

He grinned. 'Dowries are for them as wants 'em.'

They spoke little on the walk back, each one easy in the other one's company. At the clearing, his horse did as he'd done before, raised his head from eating and watched them go past without the slightest concern.

The wind was cold. It put the colt

in a playful mood, it ran at its mother, butted her, spun and kicked. She got clear from long habit.

He said, 'We'd best hurry puttin' up the hay,' and she grinned as they entered the house.

The fire was down to coals; he fed a couple of drywood scantlings to make it come back to life and Caitlin came to stand beside him.

He was leaning to kiss her, this time not on the cheek, when they both heard a shout.

12

End of a Trail

Dexter didn't recognize the voice that had called. He buckled on his shellbelt and holstered sidearm, blew out the lamp and the candles and went to the door.

Behind him, Caitlin went after the shotgun and was ready when he opened the door.

There were three of them bundled against the cold. Two of them had booted carbines, the third was slightly ahead of the other two. In poor light his face was set in stone. He had dark eyes and a wide mouth. He loosened his reins, leaned and said, 'Evenin'. I'm lookin' for a woman named Caitlin Rourke.'

Dexter stepped out into the cold, eased the door closed at his back and failed to notice that the wind had stopped.

The three strangers sat their saddles seemingly waiting for him to speak. He obliged them.

'Who are you?'

The blocky man, made blockier by his bad-weather rider's coat answered. 'My name's Carl Ames. Is she here, mister?'

Dexter didn't answer the question. Instead he said, 'Shed your guns an' come inside out of the cold.'

The older, stockier man hesitated only briefly, then swung to the ground. Behind him the other two horsemen also dismounted. They were rough men who watched Dexter like hawks without speaking. None of them shed their weapons until the older man said, 'It's not mannerly, is it?' and dropped his six-gun. The rangemen did the same.

Carl Ames looked for a place to tether his animal, found nothing close and handed the reins to the nearest rangeman.

Dexter swung the door wide, waited until Ames and the other rangeman were inside, then closed the door. The strangers stood still until two candles were lighted, then the stocky man looked steadily and impassively at the person who had made the light and Caitlin looked back.

Dexter's impression of the older man was that nothing could surprise him, and he was right. Ames was stuffing gloves into the pockets of his coat when he said, 'In your boots I'd have gone north into Canada.'

Caitlin spoke in a mildly stiff but fearless tone when she asked if the visitors would like coffee. The older man nodded, went to the table and sat. His companion did the same, the only change in the rangeman's expression was the way his eyes moved.

As Caitlin was bringing cups and the pot, the second rangeman came in, looked at Dexter and said, 'Frost before mornin'.'

Dexter did not reply.

Caitlin got another cup, filled it and put it in front of the rangeman who had just entered. The silence was awkward. She made no attempt to break it until her father-in-law said, 'You picked a good place; anyone comin' up the trail in daylight'd be visible.'

Her answer was quick. 'Is that why you came after dark?'

Ames cuddled the hot cup in both hands to soften stiff fingers. 'Caitlin, you got any idea why I wanted to find you?'

Her answer was distant. 'Yes.'

Ames slowly shook his head. 'Jess? Girl, a man can't raise a boy an' not know what he'll turn into, no matter what a father does to change that.' Ames tasted the coffee, put the cup down and spoke again. 'Are you settled here?' he asked, and when she nodded stiffly without speaking he also said, 'From what I could make out it's right nice spot, meadow, stout log house an' all. Did this gent help you?'

Dexter spoke for the first time since

they'd come inside. 'She did it all herself. I didn't meet her until last spring.'

Ames put his dark gaze on Dexter for as long as was required to make an assessment then faced the tall woman again. Whatever his next words were to be he didn't get a chance to say them. Someone hit the door from the outside, it swung all the way back to the wall and three men came in out of the cold with guns in their fists. The town blacksmith flung a gun on the floor as he addressed the three startled strangers. 'You lose somethin', mister?'

Two other hand guns skittered across the floor as the preacher threw one and Arnie Buscomb threw the third one.

Carl Ames was only very briefly startled. He recovered before the others and calmly said, 'Come in. Close the door, you're lettin' in the cold.'

The storekeeper pulled the door off the wall and closed it. He did this with his left hand, still holding the pistol in his right hand.

Ames looked at Caitlin. 'You got good neighbours,' and emptied his coffee cup, put it aside and addressed the blacksmith without blinking. 'We were havin' a sort of private talk, gents.'

The preacher replied, 'We're family, Mister Ames,' and glanced enquiringly at Caitlin. She neither spoke nor nodded. The preacher leathered the gun under his long coat and went to the fire to hold out both hands.

The blacksmith looked enquiringly at Dexter, who shrugged. Caitlin said, 'I'll make another pot of coffee.'

As she went to the stove, Carl Ames unbuttoned his coat and addressed the bull-necked blacksmith. 'Are you gents vigilantes?'

Muller replied curtly, 'When we got to be. Mister, if you come for trouble step outside an' we'll give you all you can handle with guns or without 'em.'

Ames seemed almost placid as he

considered the blacksmith. 'You boys followed us from town?'

The storekeeper answered. 'An' for as long as you've been down there. Mister, you try'n take her back.'

'I didn't come to take her back unless she wants to go back,' the dark-eyed man told the storekeeper. 'You boys are goin' to melt if you don't shed them coats.'

For a moment the only sound was of coffee boiling. Dexter and the townsmen were stunned into silence. Carl Ames twisted toward Caitlin and said, 'I didn't want Jess to marry you.'

She answered without looking from the cups she was filling. 'I knew that. Jess threw it at me often enough. He said you wanted him to marry someone better who'd bring a dowry.'

She crossed to hand the townsmen cups of hot coffee and, when she turned, avoided looking at the older man. She looked at Dexter. He winked and she winked back. Carl

Ames saw them do that, shoved out thick legs, leaned with his elbows for support against the table and said, 'Caitlin . . . ?'

She faced him. 'Yes.'

'I didn't figure to say this in front of a room full of strangers. The reason I didn't want him to marry you was because I wanted to. That's why I spent two months trying to find you.'

Except for a light wind scrabbling along the eaves outside it was quiet enough inside to hear a pin drop.

She turned slowly back toward the stove. The townsmen were embarrassed. Dexter considered the older man, went to the cot and sank down on the edge of it.

Ames arose, pulled on his gloves, buttoned his coat and spoke for the last time to Caitlin Rourke. He fished in a pocket, brought forth a worn gold ring and put it on the table. 'You knew my wife.'

'Yes. Very well.'

'She was a wonderful woman.' Ames

looked into the fireplace. 'You'll get married. I'd take it as a personal favour if you'd use her ring.'

Caitlin faced slowly away from the stove, silent and solemn.

Ames jerked his head, the rangemen arose, buttoned up and followed him out into the cold. He sent one of them for the horses about the time the preacher came out, went up beside the older man and asked a question. 'Do you believe in prayer, Mister Ames?'

The older man put a hard look on the preacher. 'Not since my wife died. I prayed all night. She died in the morning.'

'I'm sorry, Mister Ames . . . it was God's will.'

'I've heard that before, mister. Of all the miserable sons of bitches on this earth whose time it was, why her?'

The rangeman brought up the horses. Carl Ames mounted, evened up his reins and looked down at the preacher. 'What sort of man is Dexter?'

'A good man, Mister Ames. They

don't come any better.'

'I hope so, friend, I'd hate to make the long ride down here to kill him.'

Ames nodded, he and his companions crossed out of sight southward. The wind was dying, the sky was blue-black clear. Somewhere a horse stamped impatiently. The minister went back inside. He missed out on the brandy. The bottle was empty.

Caitlin said they could bed down and leave in the morning. It was an appealing idea particularly to the storekeeper who was unaccustomed to horsebacking even in daylight, but the blacksmith said he had wheels to warp on to tyres in the morning and led the way outside. The wind was down to a whisper. Little more was said as the townsmen left the clearing, but each of them had thoughts.

Dexter stood with Caitlin as long as they could hear departing riders then returned to the house where Dexter lighted the ceiling lamp and Caitlin said, 'You shouldn't use a chair.

There's a ladder out in the . . . '

'Lady,' Dexter said, as he climbed down, 'I've heard it said that when folks get married the woman promises to obey the husband, not the other way around. Are you hungry, I sure am.'

She looked steadily at him when she said, 'Yes, master, right away.'

It was too close to dawn for sleeping and the mare let them know when she lustily blew her nose before making her hungry call.

He went to feed the corralled animals. His horse was lying down with his front legs tucked under like a dog, asleep. When he returned Caitlin had breakfast ready, all but coffee. She told him there was no more, that she'd have to go down yonder to the store.

He told her to make a list and give it to him, he'd go. Her eyes widened. 'I'm up to it. I've done it for . . . '

'Not for a spell you don't. I'll tell you something else, ma'am. I know a man in Winchester who has a pair of sixteen-hundred-pound Belgian horses and a wide scraper. When he's through we'll have a regular road from here down an' back.' When she would have spoken he held up a hand. 'I know where there's a real sound dray wagon. When the road's finished an' we go to town it'll be the way folks should haul things.'

She was quiet until the meal was finished, then she said, 'Those things'll cost money.'

He agreed. 'I've got savings.'

'I didn't know I agreed to marry a rich man. Do you expect we could afford one of those glass windows to replace the one I made of scraped rawhide?'

'And maybe a dress for you.'

'Lex, while the preacher was here we could've had him . . . '

'When the road's in an' the wagon's up here, we'll go down yonder, find you the best marryin' clothes in Winchester, then go see the preacher.'

She picked up the worn gold band her father-in-law had left. 'You would have liked her, Lex. Sometimes I wondered how Jess could have turned out like he did.'

She handed him the wide, worn golden ring and while turning it in his fingers he said, 'The old man was fond of her.'

'Everyone was. As for him; I told you how he sent me that silver bracelet. I know in business he was a hard man . . . I had no idea . . . maybe I should have had. All I knew was that he was kindly toward me an' what some folks said about him.' She paused to look across the table and he smiled.

She gave him the list and he rode down to Winchester. Rebecca Buscomb was at the store, fretting, her husband had gone up-country fishing. She sighed. 'On the sly I hired a friend to go with him.' When Dexter handed her the list she only glanced at it before saying, 'That's a heap to pack on one horse,' and he agreed that it surely was, left the store to hunt up the liveryman, found him with the preacher. The liveryman asked if he wanted his horse looked after and Dexter shook his head as he asked a question. 'How sound is that dray wagon you got in the shed across the alley?'

The liveryman was a horse trader. By instinct he was also shrewd. He said, 'Nothin' wrong with it. I been thinkin' of peddlin' it.'

'For how much?'

'Well, it's sound, the wheels been oiled against shrinkin' an' the tyres is practically new. I had 'em put on about six years ago. What would you want a wagon for? The road up yonder's only a trail.'

'How much?'

'Marshal it's as good a rig as I ever owned. Don't hire it out much. Sixty dollars?'

The minister coughed and cleared his throat. The liveryman said, 'Forty dollars flat out.'

'An' a set of light harness.'

The liveryman looked pained. 'Twenty . . . '

The preacher had another coughing fit.

'Ten dollars. Marshal, you drive a hard bargain.'

Dexter counted out the greenbacks and handed them over. 'Keep it here for a spell. I've some scraper work to do.'

He and the preacher left the barn together. When they walked northward until they were opposite the emporium, the preacher said, 'Lex, in my profession a man learns to be discreet. Are you'n the tall woman goin' to marry?'

Dexter slapped the other man lightly on the shoulder as he turned to cross the road. 'I'll let you know when.'

At the store, Rebecca Buscomb wouldn't take a cent in payment. She said, 'Arnold's troublesome at times. He's given me most of my grey hair, but this is his store an' he said your friend up yonder doesn't have to pay, an' his word is the law.'

As Dexter was loading his horse he wondered about Rebecca Buscomb's last words to him.

Near the north end of town he reined in the direction of a warped and unpainted house with a large corral out back and a carelessly parked assortment of horse-drawn equipment.

The man sprawled in an old chair on the porch was chewing a cud the way only lifelong chewers did, with slow, methodical movement of his jaws. His name was Henry Lipton. He did any kind of equipment work he could get. When Dexter explained what he wanted done and asked about how much it would cost, Henry Lipton jettisoned his cud, squinted hard at the ground and eventually said, 'Fifty dollars, Marshal, an' before you scream like a wounded eagle, think how far I got to go. Forth an' back.'

Dexter said, 'When, Henry?'

'Right soon.'

'How soon is that?'

'Day after tomorrer?'

Dexter left the paunchy man heading north and a little west. He couldn't make good time, not the way his horse was loaded, but he squinted toward Forest Mountain. Caitlin would be surprised. He'd bought her a lady's blouse and some toilet water that smelled like ten days in a house of ill-repute.

Dusk was approaching when he started up the trail. He took his time in order to have every foot of the trail in mind. There were bends and crooks where Caitlin had sashayed around big rocks. When he came into the trees and could see the clearing he got a surprise. Caitlin had the mare and colt out in the meadow. The colt had never experienced such freedom. It raced almost to the northward trees before fish-tailing and racing back. Dexter could hear Caitlin laugh. The mare was cropping grass as any animal would that had been able to eat only hay for months. She paid little attention to her baby and none at all to Caitlin, but she picked the horse-sweat scent of Dexter's animal before it and its rider got clear of the trees.

Caitlin jumped up following the direction of the mare's pointing ears. She waved and left the meadow in order to meet him at the cabin. She was radiant.

He dismounted, held her close, they kissed, then he unloaded, led the horse out a ways, hobbled it and returned. Caitlin was holding up a blouse when he entered. She had emptied the saddle-bags, had put the small carton of perfume to one side and turned when he came in.

He said, 'If it don't fit it's Rebecca Buscomb's fault.' Caitlin went to the bedroom to try on the shirt and reappeared in the bedroom doorway. It was a perfect fit.

He opened the small box, unstoppered the bottle and held it toward her. She smelled the perfume, got teary eyed and told him it was the first bottle of perfume she had ever owned.

With night coming, he made a fire, heard the mare squeal and smiled. She would still be protective of the growing colt; his horse had gotten too close, a natural, but incorrect supposition.

Caitlin was putting food on the table, Dexter was shedding his shellbelt and holstered sidearm when the mare squealed again, this time in clear and obvious anger.

Dexter listened. Caitlin was busy at the table. She had done what she'd told him not to do, stand on a chair to light the overhead lamp.

He pushed the six-gun into the front of his britches and had the door open when she turned. He said, 'Coyotes most likely,' and closed the door after himself. Caitlin sobered. There were cougars and bears. There had been wolves, too but she hadn't seen a wolf in about a year. They were night animals, the others weren't.

Dexter only got as far as the corral when he saw the man inside the corral off-saddling. Visibility was poor, about all he could initially make out was that the man was lithe, and probably young.

He kept the house backgrounding him as he approached the corral, was fairly close when the off-saddled horse threw up its head and the man turned.

Dexter said, 'Good evenin'.'

The stranger returned the greeting, saw Dexter's gun in front and came to the stringers as he spoke. 'I got lost, smelt smoke and followed my nose. Didn't mean to upset no one. My name's Bob Tilman. I'm lookin' for a place called Winchester.'

Bob Tilman wrinkled his nose. 'Run out of jerky yestiddy. Be glad to pay for some hay for the horse an' somethin' to eat.'

Dexter waited until hay had been pitched to the horse then took the youthful stranger to the house.

Caitlin reacted as she usually did with strangers. She acknowledged Dexter's introduction with a nod. The stranger repeated what he'd told Dexter at the corral. Caitlin said, 'Set, I'll get you something to eat.'

By lamplight the stranger tossed his

hat aside, sat at the table and smiled at Dexter. 'I come on to that mountain, figured I'd cross it an' Winchester'd be on the other side. That mountain . . . I been crossin' it since mornin'. Would you know where Winchester is?'

Dexter was replacing his Colt in its holster on a wall peg when he answered. 'It's about nine, ten miles south an' a tad west. You can't miss it. There's no other settlement.'

Caitlin brought a platter of food and hot coffee. The youth, obviously a rangeman, looked up smiling. 'I'm sure obliged. Until I found this place I figured I'd be eatin' boot leather.'

While the stranger ate, Dexter and Caitlin exchanged glances. She shrugged and Dexter nodded, went around to the far side of the table, sat opposite the hungry man and asked where he came from.

The answer was delayed until the rangeman swallowed, washed it down with coffee then said, 'Up north. I been ridin' hard for more'n a week, had to change horses twice. Mister Ames's range boss sent me to find him. The range boss got a letter some time back sayin' Mister Ames was headin' for a place called Winchester.'

The rangeman thanked Caitlin when she put coffee in front of him then went back to the cooking area.

Dexter was holding a cup when he asked another question. 'You been ridin' hard all that time to find Mister Ames. Why?'

The rangeman pushed his empty platter aside and reached for his coffee when he replied. 'We was raided hard about ten days or so ago. Cow thieves run off better'n a hunnert head. Clint, the range boss sent me to find Mister Ames an' tell him while Clint goes after the cow thieves.'

Caitlin spoke for the first time from over by the stove. 'A hundred head? From the home place or the other ranch he owns?'

'From the home place, ma'am.'

Caitlin spoke again. 'He was here

254

yesterday. He might still be in Winchester. I think he was heading back. If you miss him you'll have another long ride.'

The rangeman looked from the tall woman to Dexter. 'You folks know Mister Ames? I'll be damned.' His surprise was genuine.

Caitlin spoke again. 'If you get to Winchester before morning you might find him.'

The rangeman stood up looking from one of them to the other. As he reached for his worn old hat he said, 'I'm right obliged. Ma'am, I'll be happy to pay for the meal an' the hay for my horse.'

Caitlin smiled slightly. 'You're welcome to them both. You better hurry.'

Dexter went to the corral as the rangeman rigged out his animal, which looked much better than it had looked earlier. As he led it out of the corral Dexter said, 'It's no more'n maybe ten miles. You'll see lights. I wouldn't push that horse, you'll get there in plenty of time.'

The younger man stepped across leather and broadly smiled. 'Just pure damned luck I smelled smoke a couple of hours ago.' He leaned and extended a hand. Dexter gripped it and released it, pointed and said, 'Through the timber for a mile or so. There's a trail eastward. It'll take you to Winchester.'

He stood in the chill until the rider was lost in darkness then returned to the house where Caitlin was doing what upset women commonly did, she was busy cleaning up after the meal, lingering in the area of her stove.

She turned. Her expression was solemn. 'Dexter, this is a big mountain. How he happened to come along this close I'll never understand. He could have ridden easterly or westerly an' missed us altogether.'

She was inwardly wound tight. She reached for her coat as she said, 'Walk with me.'

They left the cabin, were braced by

pure cold mountain air and went out where his horse and her two animals were standing hip-shot dozing. The mare had made the adjustment; it wasn't as though his horse was strange to her.

The colt saw them first and softly nickered. Dexter stood back as Caitlin and the colt met. It nuzzled her and she scratched it.

The mare turned to watch, shifted weight from one hind leg to the other and went back to dozing.

Caitlin straightened up as the colt went toward its mother. She turned. In weak starlight he saw her smile.

The rangeman's arrival hadn't worried him but it had upset her and that was understandable.

On their stroll back, holding hands, he said, 'You're an easy person to like, did you know that?'

She didn't answer, she went up against him without making a sound. It was too dark to see teary eyes.

RIDERS OF RIFLE RANGE
Wade Hamilton

Veterinarian Jeff Jones did not like open warfare — but it was there on Scrub Pine grass. When he diagnosed a sick bull on the Endicott ranch as having the contagious blackleg disease, he got involved in the warfare — whether he liked it or not!

BEAR PAW
Nevada Carter

Austin Dailey traded two cows to a pair of Indians for a bay horse, which subsequently disappeared. Tracks led to a secret hideout of fugitive Indians — and cattle thieves. Indians and stockmen co-operated against the rustlers. But it was Pale Woman who acted as interpreter between her people and the rangemen.

THE WEST WITCH
Lance Howard

Detective Quinton Hilcrest journeys west, seeking the Black Hood Bandits' lost fortune. Within hours of arriving in Hags Bend, he is fighting for his life, ensnared with a beautiful outcast the town claims is a witch! Can he save the young woman from the angry mob?

GUNS OF THE PONY EXPRESS
T. M. Dolan

Rich Zennor joined the Pony Express venture at the start, as second-in-command to tough Denning Hartman. But Zennor had the problems of Hartman believing that they had crossed trails in the past, and the fact that he was strongly attached to Hartman's Indian girl, Conchita.

BLACK JO OF THE PECOS
Jeff Blaine

Nobody knew where Black Josephine Callard came from or whither she returned. Deputy U.S. Marshal Frank Haggard would have to exercise all his cunning and ability to stay alive before he could defeat her highly successful gang and solve the mystery.

RIDE FOR YOUR LIFE
Johnny Mack Bride

They rode west, hoping for a new start. Then they met another broken-down casualty of war, and he had a plan that might deliver them from despair. But the only men who would attempt it would be the truly brave — or the desperate. They were both.

THE NIGHTHAWK
Charles Burnham

While John Baxter sat looking at the ruin that arsonists had made of his log house, a stranger rode into the yard. Baxter and Walt Showalter partnered up and re-built the house. But when it was dynamited, they struck back — and all hell broke loose.

MAVERICK PREACHER
M. Duggan

Clay Purnell was hopeful that his posting to Capra would be peaceable enough. However, on his very first day in town he rode into trouble. Although loath to use his .45, Clay found he had little choice — and his likeness to a notorious bank robber didn't help either!

SIXGUN SHOWDOWN
Art Flynn

After years as a lawman elsewhere, Dan Herrick returned to his old Arizona stamping ground to find that nesters were being driven from their homesteads by ruthless ranchers. Before putting away his gun once and for all, Dan forced a bloody and decisive showdown.

RIDE LIKE THE DEVIL!
Sam Gort

Ben Trunch arrived back on the Big T only to find that land-grabbing was in progress. He confronted Luke Fletcher, saloon-keeper and town boss, with what was happening, and was immediately forced to ride for his life. But he got the chance to put it all right in the end.

SLOW WOLF AND DAN FOX:
Larry & Stretch
Marshall Grover

The deck was stacked against an innocent man. Larry Valentine played detective, and his investigation propelled the Texas Trouble-Shooters into a gun-blazing fight to the finish.

BRANAGAN'S LAW
Alan Irwin

To Angus Flint, the valley was his domain and he didn't want any new settlers. But Texas Ranger Jim Branagan had other ideas. Could he put an end to Flint's tyranny for good?

THE DEVIL RODE A PINTO
Bret Rey

When a settler is cut to ribbons in a frenzied attack, Texas Ranger Sam Buck learns that the killer is Rufus Berry, known as The Devil. Sam stiffens his resolve to kill or capture Berry and break up his gang.

THE DEATH MAN
Lee F. Gregson
The hardest of men went in fear of Ford, the bounty hunter, who had earned the name 'The Death Man'. Yet even Ford was not infallible — when he killed the wrong man, he found that he was being sought himself by the feared Frank Ambler.

LEAD LANGUAGE
Gene Tuttle
After Blaze Colton and Ricky Rawlings have delivered a train load of cows from Arizona to San Francisco, they become involved in a load of trouble and find themselves on the run!

A DOLLAR FROM THE STAGE
Bill Morrison
Young saddle-tramp Len Finch stumbled into a web of murder, lawlessness, intrigue and evil ambition. In the end, he put his life on the line for the folks that he cared about.

BRAND 2: HARDCASE
Neil Hunter

When Ben Wyatt and his gang hold up the bank in Adobe, Wyatt is captured. Judge Rice asks Jason Brand, an ex-U.S. Marshal, to take up the silver star. Wyatt is in the cells, his men close by, and Brand is the only man to get Adobe out of real trouble . . .

THE GUNMAN AND THE ACTRESS
Chap O'Keefe

To be paid a heap of money just for protecting a fancy French actress and her troupe of players didn't seem that difficult — but Joshua Dillard hadn't banked on the charms of the actress, and the fact that someone didn't want him even to reach the town . . .